THINGS HOPED FOR

DERINDA BABCOCK

Cover and Interior Design: Derinda Babcock

Editor(s): Helene Smith

PUBLISHED BY: 4Him Press, P.O.Box 127, Marvel, CO 81329, 2023

Library Cataloging Data

Names: Babcock, Derinda (Derinda Babcock)

Things Hoped For / Derinda Babcock

110 p. 23cm × 15cm (9in × 6 in.)

Identifiers: ISBN-13: 979-8-9893327-6-2 (paperback) | 979-8-9893327-8-6 (trade paperback) | 979-8-9893327-9-3 (hardback) | 979-8-9893327-7-9 (e-book)

Key Words: clean and wholesome romance; cowboy romance Christian; rancher romance books; mountain survival; search and rescue romance; love and relationships; western romance

Library of Congress Control Number: 2024916350 Fiction

Now faith is the substance of things hoped for,
the evidence of things not seen.
Hebrews 11:1 (KJV)

CHAPTER 1

BRIAN MORGAN whistled to the dogs and wheeled his horse to cut off a couple of breakaway steers and head them back to the herd. He swung his lariat. "Get up, cows."

The irritation in his voice matched the frustration roiling his gut, tightening his jaw, and fisting his gloved hands. What a way to spend his thirtieth birthday—sorting, deworming, branding, castrating, and moving cattle to their summer range. Though he and his family always moved cows in the spring, he wanted something different.

His eyes followed the easy movements of his older brothers, Bill, Charlie, and Colton as they whistled commands to the dogs and guided their horses.

Brian's gaze lingered on Colton. Ever since his brother and sister-in-law, Belle, were rescued after their plane crashed in the Colorado Rockies seven months ago, his discontent flared. Their lives seemed so much richer and more exciting than his.

From the moment he discovered Colton in the hospital bed with his arms around a sleeping Belle, his unrest grew.

How had a rough-around-the-edges Montana cowboy like Colton ended up with an elegant and sophisticated heiress from Dallas? His mind boggled at the thought.

Brian's eyes slid to his right and rested on Belle. His parents, sisters-in-law, nieces, nephews, and a couple of neighbors worked the cattle from horseback, but Colton had insisted Belle drive the side by side containing food, water, the first aid kit, and equipment. Though Belle rode well, Colton said he would not chance anything happening to her or their unborn child.

Belle seemed content with her life on the ranch, but Brian didn't understand how she could be. He'd stayed in the St. Johns' luxurious penthouse in Dallas and admired the rich and famous people who attended the glittering reception her parents held for Belle and Colton in January. He had enjoyed the fast-paced lifestyle he'd lived during this time.

Returning to the ranch to deal with ornery cattle, ongoing equipment repair, fencing, wood hauling, horseshoeing, and the other thousands of mundane things required to maintain a ranch pained his soul.

Belle must have felt his gaze. She turned and smiled at him, a question in her eyes.

His lips tightened, and he looked away. He heeled his horse until he rode beside a neighbor and long-time friend, Juliette Blackhawk.

She turned her dark, slightly almond-shaped eyes on him and scanned his expression and body language. "Why are you on the prod?"

"What makes you think I am, Jules?"

She snorted and focused on the cattle.

He grimaced. "I guess I am, a little. Do you ever wish you could get away and do something different?"

Juliette turned her full attention on him. "Of course. Why do you think I left for two years?"

Brian shrugged. "I didn't know if you did because you felt trapped, or because you followed some ritual from your Native American ancestors I never knew about."

"You're serious?" She chuckled. Her wide, attractive smile held his attention. "My family has intermarried with Whites for so long, I don't think they remember any of the traditions. Some tribal members call us coconuts."

Brian frowned. "Coconuts?"

She chuckled again. "Yes—people who are brown on the outside, but white on the inside."

Regardless of what others called Jules, no one could ignore how attractive she was, even dressed in denim and leather work clothes, boots, and a wide-brimmed felt hat. More notable than her appearance, though, was her down-to-earth personality. She was easy to be with.

"So, why did you leave for two years? Where did you go? When I asked your relatives, they gave me vague answers."

She shrugged. "They were upset I left. They didn't understand why I wasn't content with what I had."

Brian's heartbeat increased. "Where did you go?"

"I went to New York City and got a job modeling."

"Why New York City?"

"The place was as far away from Montana as I could think of."

Brian pondered her answer. "You came home."

"Yes, but only after I truly discovered what I wanted from life. I realized I had to sacrifice certain things in order to have others. I made a lot of money as a model, but I gave up clean air and mountains for the rat race, crime, and violence of the city. These got to me after a while."

She searched his face. "If you left, what would you do? Do you have marketable skills other than ranching?"

Brian sighed. "I don't think so." *I'll be stuck here forever.*

Over the next four days of the cattle drive, he pondered Juliette's question.

What skills did he have? He knew cattle, horses, dogs, hunters, and butchering. He could build fences and repair tractors and other machinery that always seemed to break down at one point or another. But every other rancher and his hands had the same skills.

He was not as unique as his brothers. Bill had developed exceptional photography and videography skills which were in high demand with wildlife magazines and wedding planners. When he wasn't ranching or hunting, he made a good income with his photography, especially after Belle sent some of her and Colton's wedding pictures he'd taken to the news reporter who had interviewed them after the crash. The images went viral.

Charlie wrote articles for hunting magazines and farming and ranching trade journals. When his wife, Grace, wanted to create a book to show others how to forage plants in the wild, Charlie wrote the book with Grace's guidance, and Bill photographed the plants.

The book, though published two years ago, continued to bring in a steady income stream, especially with the extra videos and info they provided on social media.

Grace, Laura, and Belle had bonded from the first moment they'd met, and they now planned another book utilizing their skills in foraging and using wild plants in food preparation.

This book was sure to be a hit just because people showed continued fascination with Belle's survival story and the promise of more details when her book, *Belle and the Mountain Man: An Unlikely Romance*, released in six months.

Colton was much like him in many ways. They had similar mountain and cattle ranching abilities, but they hadn't developed any extra skills—not like Bill and Charlie.

Except my oil paintings.

Brian pushed this thought away. What good to him was the ability to paint well? Sure, the process relaxed him, but he had no confidence he was good enough to make a living at oil painting. He understood the implications of the phrase 'starving artist' and had no intention of joining their numbers.

Colton's ability to win the heart of someone like Belle still disturbed him. How had he done this? Colton didn't enjoy people and new things as well as he did, so what attracted Belle to Colton?

He had a chance to ask her the next morning. When he came down to the kitchen before dawn, Belle had just placed a delicious-looking casserole in the oven. She turned around and brushed her hands over her apron.

Her eyes met his. "Are you ready to talk now instead of running?"

He sat at the counter, and she poured him a cup of coffee. He wanted to object, but didn't. She was right.

Brian stared at the steaming liquid before raising his eyes. "Why did you choose Colton? You both come from vastly different environments, and I can't understand how this happened."

Her eyebrows raised, and she opened her mouth to answer, but Colton came in from feeding the animals.

He smiled and embraced her. "I want to know the same thing, sweetheart. We never made sense together, yet, here we are." He caressed Belle's middle.

She kissed him and indicated with a head tilt he should sit next to Brian.

Brian waited as she poured Colton a cup of coffee.

Belle studied his brother. "I misjudged him at first and made faulty assumptions based on past experiences with other people. I didn't realize I'd made such a grave error in judgment until he explained his thinking and ..." she paused and smiled, remembering in her eyes.

Colton finished her sentence. "I kissed her. I had to. She made me crazy."

Brian grinned. "I haven't heard that part."

Belle chuckled. "No one will until Amber Morris finishes the book. Colton kissed me and stirred emotions I didn't recognize. I pushed them to the back of my mind."

"I don't know what she thought when I kissed her on such short acquaintance." Colton chuckled. "She didn't slap me, so I'm glad I took a chance."

"As we struggled to live, I was afraid and anxious. When I laid my head on Colton's shoulder at night, his scent and heartbeat made me feel safe, and his warmth comforted me. My love for him grew as the days passed."

"Ah. That's why I found you sleeping in his arms when we came to the hospital."

Belle nodded.

Brian's eyes met hers. "Do you miss the fast-paced excitement of city life?"

"Not often. With a husband like Colton and a family like I have now, every day is filled with joy and interesting things to do. If I want to return to the city, I can, but I won't stay long. My life is here."

Brian blinked. He couldn't process her words. The ranch was exciting? Colton was exciting?

Belle stared at him as if she could read his soul. "You're not happy here, are you?"

Colton straightened and turned to him.

Brian grimaced. "How did you know?"

"I recognized the same discontent in my life after I met Colton. I probably wore the same expression that you now wear when I was away from him."

Colton frowned. "You're an important part of what we do, Brian. If you leave—"

Brian held up a hand. "*When* I leave, you can hire someone to take my place."

Colton shook his head. "Won't be the same. You're family."

Brian cocked his head. "Family is important to me too, but I'll go crazy if I don't do something different soon. I'm suffocating here."

Belle touched his hand. “What will you do?”

Brian released a heavy sigh. “That is the frustrating part. I don’t have any other marketable skills outside of ranching and guiding. Leaving this place would mean I’d have to work on another ranch to make a living.”

Colton rested both arms on the counter. “What different skills do you wish you had?”

Brian shrugged. “I don’t know. Something interesting that would allow me to enjoy a faster-paced life with the ability to talk to someone other than family and cantankerous cows. But I’m a realist. I’m thirty years old, Colton. When and how would I learn such skills?”

Belle checked the casserole in the oven. “Many older people go to college. You could do this too.”

Brian’s laugh wasn’t humorous. “I haven’t done bookwork or studied since I finished my Associate of Science degree thirteen years ago, Belle. I can visualize me trying to get back into the swing of studying and taking tests. Not a pretty picture.”

Belle turned back to him. “If you knew what you wanted to do, I could help you with the academics. I’ve been out of school a few years, but I was an excellent student.”

“Thank you. I’ll keep your offer in mind if I figure out what I want to do.” Brian’s heart warmed to her. He appreciated her willingness to help.

Whining and scratching signaled Mindy’s desire to enter.

Belle opened the door, and the border collie slipped in and sat at Brian’s feet. She waited expectantly for him to acknowledge her.

He scratched her head, then glanced between Belle and Colton. "Enough about me. What other interesting tidbits will come to light when Amber Morris finishes your story? I'm all ears."

Belle laughed. "I guess you'll just have to wait and see, brother. Amber is coming to the ranch on Monday to work. She has only a chapter or two to finish."

"Will I show up in any of the narrative?"

"Of course. Your first appearance will be standing at the side of Colton's hospital bed with your parents."

Someone called Colton's phone. He looked at the number and answered. "Adam? Hang on. Let me put you on speaker. Belle's here."

"Hey, girlfriend. How are you? Colton, Liam and I thought we'd stop by for a visit if you have room. I'm between flights, and Liam is between concerts."

Colton smiled. "Of course. When?"

"Monday. The airline offered specials, so we took advantage of this. We'll rent a car and drive to your place. We can stay five days."

"Great. See you then." Colton hung up. "We'll have a houseful, but we have plenty of room."

At that moment, Belle's cell rang. She raised her eyebrows at the number, then answered. "Mr. Willis. How are you? Let me put you on speaker. Colton is here."

Randy Willis's excited voice filled the room. "So glad you're both able to hear me. We'll wrap up filming of your plane crash story soon and finish the edits, then we'll move to postproduction.

"I need a little more information before we do. I want to show you both what we have. Do you have room at the ranch for me and a couple of videographers for a few days?"

Belle raised her eyebrows. Colton nodded and mouthed, "They can stay in the bunkhouse."

Brian smiled. Life had suddenly gotten interesting.

Belle's eyes sparkled. "We have room for you, Mr. Willis. When will you arrive?"

"Our flight gets in Monday afternoon. We'll rent a car."

Belle laughed. "Watch for Liam and Adam. They're arriving about the same time."

"Now that is exceptional news. I wanted to speak to them too. This will save me extra trips."

Colton leaned closer to the speaker. "We'll let the family know to expect you. See you on Monday." Belle hung up, then grinned at Brian. "You were saying something about the ranch being slow-paced?"

He laughed. "I stand corrected. At least this next week promises to be entertaining."

CHAPTER 2

BRIAN sniffed the wonderful aroma of baking and roasting issuing from the kitchen early Monday morning. His stomach rumbled and his mouth watered, but the only time he'd tried to enter the kitchen to pinch a hot roll, his mom threatened him with a wooden spoon.

Just after daylight, the women put breakfast out. They all sat around the large table and made sure everything was ready for their guests.

"Mom, who is staying where?" Laura smeared fresh butter on her roll.

Janet reached for the scrambled eggs. "Miss Morris will stay in the front guest room. Adam and Liam will stay next to her. Belle and Miss Morris can use the third extra bedroom as an office if they want. We'll put Mr. Willis and his friends in the bunkhouse where the hunters usually stay. All the sheets are freshly laundered and the beds made, so all we have to do is finish planning the rest of the meals and the entertainment."

Brian eyed his mother. Her flushed cheeks and smiling eyes caused him to wonder if she liked excitement too. He'd never thought about anyone else's need for new things to keep life fun.

Amber Morris arrived before noon. Mom had put Brian in charge of greeting the guests and helping with the luggage. As soon as he saw the elegant, sophisticated woman get out of her rental car, his breath hitched. Her light brown hair shone. She was as beautiful as Belle.

He smiled. "Welcome to the Morgan Ranch, Miss Morris. Let me help you with your bags."

Her matching smile made his heart pound behind his ribs. "Call me, Amber."

"I'm Brian."

She offered her hand. "Nice to meet you, Brian. I now have a face to put with a name."

Her voice was pleasant and as soft as her hand. Her light scent made him want to move closer. *Get control of yourself!* He released her hand and stepped back. "Lunch will be ready in ten minutes. Belle and my mother are waiting for you, so follow me."

Brian took her luggage to the guest room while Amber and Belle chatted downstairs. He berated himself all the way up the stairs for his instant susceptibility to beautiful women. He instinctively wanted to reach for them or for his oil brushes and paints.

Adam, Liam, Randy Willis, and his two videographers, Lewis and Joel, arrived by three o'clock. They all met in the large living room to chat before dinner. The aroma filling the house let him know his mom, Belle, Laura, and Grace were giving the guests their best efforts.

Brian eased himself into a chair out of the main sight line and watched. Every unmarried male in the room, down to his two teenaged nephews, Landon and Joseph, responded to Amber Morris the way he had.

She must have seen these reactions many times before, because she took their admiring looks in stride and gave them each warm glances.

Had their roles been reversed, Brian didn't think he would have handled the situation with as much sangfroid as Amber did.

Mom stepped into the room and waved. "Come and eat."

Brian waited for the guests to head to the dining room before following.

Colton, Bill, and Charlie carried steaming platters of food and set them in the middle of the long table.

Brian grabbed one of the pitchers and filled water glasses. He knew the routine. All Morgan hands helped when they had guests.

His nieces, Wren and Christy, handed each diner a small hand sanitizer packet from baskets they carried. Charlie's twins, Kirk and Danny, would be responsible for removing and scraping the dirty dishes and placing them in the dishwasher later.

Randy cleared his throat. "Mr. and Mrs. Morgan, may Lewis and Joel take videos? Maybe a few candid shots throughout the evening? This will give viewers a sense of Colton and Belle's life after the crash."

Henry shrugged. "I don't mind if they don't."

Amber chuckled and looked at the videographers. "Promise me you won't get us when we have our mouths open and are taking huge bites of this amazing food."

The tips of both men's ears turned red, but they nodded. They reached for their cameras, found the best shooting angles, and pushed record.

They all lingered over the meal, and the lively conversation centered on each visitor's purpose for being at the ranch.

Brian smiled at the animated faces. This was the kind of stimulating conversation he enjoyed.

Neither Randy nor Amber gave away many details of how they intended to make the survivors' stories come alive, but they dropped hints to heighten everyone's desire to hear more.

Brian glanced at Colton. He was the only one who didn't seem excited about the attention. Did a look of dread come and go in his eyes?

Belle circled her hand around his bicep and whispered something in his ear.

Colton nodded, and the tenseness left his jaw.

Adam grinned and gave Liam a knowing look before returning his attention to Randy Willis.

The moviemaker smiled. "If you all promise not to say anything to anyone outside this room, I'll show you a rough cut of the video footage before I leave. Agreed?"

"Yes!" Multiple voices spoke as one.

Mom rose. "Why don't you all return to the living room. We'll start a fire." Her eyes swung to the youngest survivor. "Liam, we have a guitar. Will you sing for us?"

Randy spoke before Liam answered. "Please sing what you sang for Belle and the others after the crash."

Liam studied Belle's face as if asking permission.

She nodded.

"All right."

Colton started the fire and lowered the lights, while Dad went upstairs to fetch the guitar.

The subtle play of emotions on Belle's and his brother's faces focused Brian's attention. She snuggled against Colton, and he put an arm around her.

He glanced at the pilot. Adam tried not to show much expression, but the muscles in his jaws flexed as if this turn of events startled him.

Brian straightened and leaned forward. Would Liam's singing stir up fresh memories? Painful memories?

The mood shifted from comfortable to serious. Amber studied the survivors' faces when Liam strummed the opening notes to the first song. Her glance met Brian's for a moment before she turned away.

Liam's eyes moved from Belle, to Colton, to Adam as he sang. He played as if they were the only ones in the room—as if he sang only to them. His eyes held a message they seemed to understand.

The videographers moved quietly and unobtrusively around the room, and Randy stared. Anyone could identify his expression as fascinated and beyond pleased.

The sound and words of Liam's songs moved Brian in a way he couldn't fathom. They left him more unsettled.

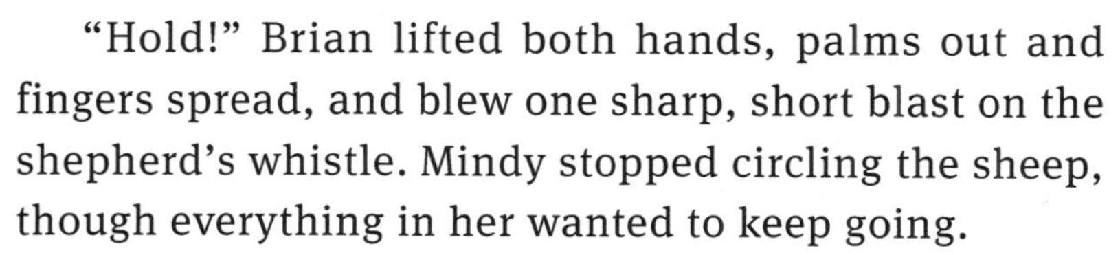

"Hold!" Brian lifted both hands, palms out and fingers spread, and blew one sharp, short blast on the shepherd's whistle. Mindy stopped circling the sheep, though everything in her wanted to keep going.

As Brian trained the border collie in the round pen, he forced himself to focus on the dog instead of what might be happening in the house. Belle and Amber worked on the last chapters, and Randy Willis and his videographers followed Colton, Adam, and Liam somewhere.

The sheep huddled against the fence and stared at the dog.

"Come by." Brian paired the voice command with the arm signal and the special three-note whistle.

Instantly, Mindy raced around the sheep and pushed them away from the fence.

"Fetch." He made another arm movement paired with a different whistle, and the dog nipped at the sheep's heels until they moved toward him.

Mindy's taut body radiated joy. She nipped enthusiastically.

"Steady." His words were a quiet warning. "Out." The collie moved away from the sheep and circled at more of a distance.

"Hold."

Mindy stopped and whined, her eyes intent on the sheep.

"Come."

At first, the dog ignored the command.

"Come." Brian gave the hand signal and the associated whistle.

Mindy turned and rushed to him for his pets of approval.

"Good girl."

"That was impressive. Your dog is well trained." Randy Willis stared at Mindy.

Brian raised his head.

The videographers lowered their cameras.

Lewis grinned. “I wish my kids were as well trained.”

Willis studied the dog. “How long have you been working with her?”

Brian scratched Mindy’s head. “Since she was nine weeks old. She’s a year and a half now and is learning to respond to whistles. These are easier to hear at a distance.”

Colton walked up and leaned his forearms on the top rail. “Brian is our dog whisperer. My brothers and I signal the border collies when we round up cattle and sheep using the same whistles, but Brian does the majority of the training.”

Bill and Charlie walked over dressed in chaps and spurs. They led their saddled horses and two more.

Colton tilted his head. “If you want to come with us, we’re checking on cattle. You can see the dogs work.”

“Absolutely.” Randy turned to Lewis and Joel. “Are you up for some horseback riding?”

They nodded.

“May we come?” Adam and Liam joined them.

Colton grinned at Adam. “Have you ridden before?”

Adam’s mouth turned up at the corners and he put on an innocent face. “A time or two. Riding is kind of like flying a plane, right? You signal your intent with hands and feet.”

Liam laughed. “Let’s hope they don’t put you on an animal that’s more like your fighter jet than a rocking horse.”

Bill and Charlie saddled more horses.

Hoofbeats approached, and they turned toward the rider.

Juliette Blackhawk stopped and scanned the group.

Brian mounted. “Hey, Jules. Want to ride with us? We’re going to check on the cattle in the north pasture. I want the dogs to practice more.”

“Sure.”

Joel whistled under his breath. “Wow. Another stunning beauty.”

Brian frowned. He didn’t like the greedy, intense way Joel gazed at Juliette, so he heeled his horse between the videographer and his friend.

When they reached the north pasture, Colton signaled Randy and his guys and Liam and Adam to stay back and watch. The videographers dismounted and raised their cameras to their shoulders.

Brian tilted his head toward the cattle. “Ready, Jules?”

Juliette reached for her lariat and nodded, and they rode with Bill, Charlie, and Colton.

They didn’t return to the ranch house until late afternoon.

Mother waited on the porch and shaded her eyes in their direction. “Jules, is that you?”

“Yes, ma’am.”

“Come in. Do you want to stay for dinner?”

“Thanks, Janet, but I’d better go. Dad will be hungry. Maybe some other time?”

“Plan on coming over for dinner the day after tomorrow around five. Mr. Willis will show us a preview of his documentary after we eat. I thought this would be a fun night to dress up and pretend we’re at the theater. We plan to move the furniture and dance.”

"All right. Thank you." Her eyes slid to Brian before she turned toward the gate.

His gaze met and held hers.

"She sure is a picture of grace and beauty." Joel lifted his camera and hit record, just as Juliette heeled the horse into a canter.

Brian's jaw tightened. He led his horse into the barn and unsaddled without saying a word to any of them.

Colton did the same, but his eyes moved from Juliette's retreating back to Brian's face, speculation raising one of his eyebrows.

Willis and his crew returned to the bunkhouse to wash, but Brian followed his brothers into the washroom just inside the front door of the ranch house.

Brian didn't want to answer the questions he saw in Colton's eyes, so he moved to the living room where Belle stared at one of his paintings.

She moved from painting to painting and leaned close to study the signature.

Would she say anything when she realized?

Belle looked up, her eyes wide. "These are yours. I admire them every time I come in here or gaze at the ones in the upstairs hall, but I never stopped to see who painted them until just now. You're better than good, brother."

He wished. "Which one do you like the best?"

Without hesitation, she pointed at the one of Colton and the other brothers herding cattle in the winter. "This one. I see the breaths of horses, cattle, and men in the cold air. I feel the snow on my face and want to snuggle in a warm blanket and drink hot chocolate. I don't know how you captured the sense of movement and cold on a flat canvas, but you did. I'm amazed. What do you call this?"

Her words soothed his earlier irritation. "I haven't named the painting."

"I'm going to call this *Belle's Favorite* then."

Throughout dinner, Brian often caught his sister-in-law watching him with a thoughtful expression. What was she thinking? He didn't trust the gleam in her eyes.

"I hear you are a dog whisperer, Brian." Amber's soft voice turned Brian's attention to her.

His heartbeat picked up speed when he looked across the table at her. "That's what they say."

"Would you mind if I watch you work tomorrow? I've been a fan of dog trials and dog shows from a young age. I promise not to distract you."

Huh. You don't have to say a word to do that, lady. Everything about you sidetracks me.

"I don't mind."

CHAPTER 3

Brian took the stairs two at a time, anticipation adding a bounce to each step. When he reached his room, he slammed the door, stripped off his boots and clothes, and headed to the shower. *What will Willis show us tonight? Will I finally get a clue as to what attracted Belle to Colton?*

He shaved, patted on aftershave, and took extra care with his hair and dress. He slid into his blue jeans, stomped on his black boots, and buttoned into his best white shirt. He looped the leather belt around his waist and hooked the large, shiny rodeo buckle he'd won in the team roping event with Colton.

Belle's words replayed themselves in his mind. She'd said Colton's scent and heartbeat made her feel safe, and his warmth comforted her.

Her words didn't help him understand. He'd slipped up next to Colton today when they'd finished chores and inhaled. All he smelled on his brother was horse, sweat, and a whiff of pine needles that habitually scented his coat. Nothing noteworthy or out of the ordinary in his opinion.

Brian figured Colton's heart beat the same way as his, so why would this make Belle feel a sense of security?

He had no trouble understanding how staying warm in a cold environment would make her comfortable, but surely, something else drew them.

He opened the door and stepped into the hall.

Colton and Belle did the same only a moment later.

Brian blinked and stared at the two, his mouth ajar. His brother had shaved and dressed in mirror-image clothing, even down to the belt buckle. He looked ... normal.

Belle, on the other hand, took his breath away. She sparkled in the light. Even her skin glowed. She wore her hair up and had chosen to dress in a sleeveless, silky red dress and matching red cowboy boots. Diamonds dripped from her earlobes, and a diamond necklace encircled her neck. The thin, glittering rhinestone belt hugged her slightly expanding middle.

"Well?" Colton's eyebrows lifted.

Brian took a deep breath and shook his head. "I'll never understand why Belle picked you."

"Neither will I. Are you jealous?"

"Yes, but seeing a cowboy like you with a woman like Belle gives a regular guy like me hope."

Colton smirked. "My wife assures me I'm special, and Bill says I'm quite photogenic." His laugh indicated he didn't quite believe what he'd been told.

Belle clasped Colton's hand. "He's still my hero and protector, Brian."

A hero and protector. Were those characteristics important? Did most independent women these days want heroes and protectors? What qualities made a man a hero? He'd have to look up the definition.

Brian had protective instincts, but he suspected he'd missed out on the hero attributes if he compared himself to returning soldiers who'd earned purple hearts. The thought depressed him.

He frowned at Colton. "You don't plan to keep her to yourself during the dancing, do you? That would be extremely unfair to the rest of us."

Belle laughed. "I'll save a dance for you."

"See that you do. I'm sure Adam and Liam will want their turns as well as our other brothers and Willis, but I have first dibs."

Colton frowned. "I'm not going to spare her for that many dances."

Brian laughed and descended the stairs in front of them.

The doorbell rang as Mom and Dad brought in trays of food. Mom tilted her head. "Will you get that, Brian?"

"Sure."

He opened the door. Juliette smiled at him, and his heart almost stopped. This wasn't his childhood friend who rode horses and worked cattle, but the woman who'd gone to New York to model.

He didn't have words to describe the soft, flowing material of her white, sleeveless dress. He only knew the combination of the dress, the white fringed cowboy boots, and her sapphire necklace and earrings made him pay attention to the softness of her skin. He fisted his hand to keep from touching.

He inhaled. "Jules. You're stunning."

Her eyes sparkled. “Thank you. Janet told me to wear something comfy enough to dance in. Am I late?”

Brian opened the door wider. “No, you’re not. Come in. We’re hanging out in the living room until everyone gets here.” He offered an elbow. “Save the first slow dance for me, okay?”

“I will.” Juliette put her hand in the bend of his arm and walked with him into the living room.

The doorbell rang again.

“Excuse me, Jules. The producer and his videographers are here. I’ll be back in a minute.”

The men stepped into the foyer just as Amber Morris glided down the stairs in a gorgeous blue dress with a fitted bodice and flared skirt. She also glittered.

“Good evening, gentlemen.” Her soft voice turned their eyes to her.

“Wow!” Joel’s hand instinctively reached for his camera.

Brian’s gut churned. How was he going to breathe with Belle, Jules, and Amber in his space all evening? He knew he was a sucker for gorgeous women, and these three were more beautiful than most. They stirred his blood and excited his artist’s eye. He hoped he wouldn’t make a fool of himself.

The appreciative looks of every male in the room, including his teen nephews, told him he wasn’t the only one in jeopardy of functioning with a scrambled brain.

Mom smiled. “All right, you all. Dinner is ready.”

They trailed into the dining room.

Food offerings that probably came from the menu of Belle’s parents’ five-star restaurants filled the center of the table. The dishes looked as enticing as the people, and Brian's stomach growled at the aroma.

Randy smiled at Belle. "I recognize the wild mushroom asparagus risotto and the lobster and crab bisque from your parents' restaurant. Are these their recipes?"

Belle smiled. "Yes. They are some of the dishes you, Adam, Liam, and I had when we met in Dallas. I've put my own touch on the prime rib. Janet made the bacon-wrapped shrimp, Laura created that delicious-looking salad, and Grace used foraged herbs to season the pork tenderloin."

Lewis and Joel took short videos and then slid into their chairs to enjoy the meal. They didn't say much, but their furtive gazes seldom left the women.

Amber sat across the table from him and next to Adam, and he could see how the writer turned her full attention on the pilot when he spoke. She looked intently interested in what he was saying.

When Liam asked her something, she turned and focused on him as if he were the only person in the room. Did she develop such skill as a listener because of her job, or because she genuinely liked people?

"She's beautiful." Juliette spoke from beside him.

Brian startled and met her eyes. "I don't know where to focus. I want to reach for my paintbrushes and oils."

She chuckled. "The other men are having the same problem, though Bill, Charlie, and Colton are keeping their gazes where they belong—on their own wives."

Brian grinned and focused on Juliette for the next hour.

They lingered over the meal, but Brian sensed when the mood changed to expectancy. They all helped with clean up and then returned to the living room.

Joel and Lewis set up a portable large screen and DVD player.

Randy made eye contact with each person, but he addressed his words to Belle, Colton, Liam, and Adam. "This is a rough cut of the documentary. I'd like you to make sure all the information we have so far is accurate.

"If we miss something you think is important, please tell us to stop the video so we can make notes. When we move into the post-production stage, we'll edit, work with the sound and visual effects, and perform color grading."

He smiled. "Getting to know you all made casting much easier. I hope you like the actors who represent you."

Liam laughed, caught Adam's eye, and leaned forward. "I really want to see this, especially the person who's playing Colton."

Brian wanted the same thing. Maybe observing how the actor portrayed his brother would give him the insight he didn't have right now.

The muscle moving in Colton's tight jaw signaled his distrust of what might come. *Is he afraid the moviemaker will reveal a secret he didn't want others to know, or does he truly dislike the attention?*

Brian suspected Colton disliked the attention more than he was afraid of a secret. He knew his brother well. Other than at rodeo events, he didn't like being in the spotlight.

For the next hour and a half, Brian watched the movie, glancing often at Colton, Belle, Adam, and Liam to see how they responded to the scenes. The actors resembled each of the four, and they could act.

He hadn't realized how serious the situation had been until he saw his family and friends struggle for every bite of food and drink of water. The hunger pains gnawed his belly, and he sensed their urgent need to get off the mountain.

As his admiration for the four grew, so did the realization that he might not be in Colton's class when heroes and protectors were chosen. How could he be? He had no opportunity to show anyone, least of all himself, what he had inside him. He grimaced.

"Will you please stop the film, Mr. Willis? I need clarification." Amber Morris studied her notes. "Colton, when Adam asked Belle if she had a boyfriend or husband, she said no. You asked if she expected to live in Dallas if she found a man who could love her for who she was and not because of her inheritance."

"Yes."

"Belle said she couldn't interpret the expression on your face when she told you she was flexible and could live in the city or the country.

"Will you tell me what you were thinking? She said you appeared to want to ask something but changed your mind."

Moments passed, and Brian wondered if Colton would answer.

The corners of his brother's mouth turned up. "I wanted to marry Belle from day one, regardless of how much money she had. I listened to her chat with one of the passengers during the flight, and her intelligence and beauty twisted my insides like I'd been gut-kicked by a bronc. I started to ask if she'd consider coming to Montana and marrying a rough-around-the-edges cowboy."

Belle turned to stare at him, her eyes wide. "You did?"

"Yes."

Brian stared. How had Colton known so quickly? The documentary hadn't shown the actors engaged in this conversation.

Amber tapped her pencil on the notepad. "And were you at the first camp or the second when you kissed Belle for the first time?"

Laura, Grace, and his mother gasped and waited for an answer. The others leaned forward, smiles and gleaming eyes showing their interest.

Colton glanced at Adam and Liam before answering. "We weren't at either camp, but we were in the area of the first. We searched for water and a way out."

Randy raised his eyebrows. "I'd like to hear this part of the story."

"We'd all like to hear." Brian grinned at Colton.

Amber held up an index finger. "Uh-uh. This info is specific to the book. If you want more details, you'll have to—"

Charlie chuckled. "Ah, come on, Miss Morris. Just a few more tidbits?"

"Please?" The others agreed in unison.

Amber shrugged and turned to Belle. "This part is yours to tell if you're going to share."

Lewis and Joel raised their cameras, but Amber shook her head at the videographers. “No video, please.”

Belle’s expression sobered. “From the first time I saw Colton, I made faulty assumptions about what he thought about me based on my interpretation of his words and actions.” She intertwined her fingers with his. “I misjudged him from the time Adam introduced us.”

Brian’s gazed moved from Colton to Belle. “What kind of faulty assumptions?”

Belle related their interactions up to the time of the kiss. “I unintentionally spoke my thoughts. I asked Colton why he disliked me so much. The way he flinched at my question, you would have thought I struck him in the back with something hard.

“He shattered my misconceptions, then he ...” she grinned and waited for Colton to finish the story.

“I kissed her. I kissed her well. She made me crazy.” His tone was matter of fact, but his eyes were soft with remembering.

Randy raised an eyebrow. “In what way?”

Colton’s jaw tightened. “The pilot and the preacher slept on each side of her and enjoyed Belle’s scent and warmth, while I stayed on the outside with a knot of jealousy souring my gut. At first, she gave them smiles, but I earned her frowns.”

Adam laughed. “Sleeping arrangements changed soon after the kiss.”

Liam grinned and nodded.

Randy stared. “What about those arrangements? In light of—”

Amber smiled. "That information, Mr. Willis, will be revealed in the book."

Juliette tilted her head. "When will the book release, Miss Morris?"

Excitement lit Amber's eyes. "As soon as I give these last two chapters to my editor on Monday, I have an excellent formatter ready to change the manuscript into book and e-book form once Belle approves the edits. We're planning an audiobook soon after. We're vetting narrators now.

"The cover is almost finished. Since Belle is independently publishing, we can get the book up within the next two months. The marketing team is ready to launch information on social media soon, and Belle and Colton have an interview on a popular national morning show within a week of the release."

Colton muttered, "Then we're going to be in for a three-ring circus."

Brian chuckled. "Are you going to hop on a horse and take to the hills, bro?"

"Huh. I wish. I'll stay with my wife and face the music."

Brian watched the rest of the movie without comment, though his thoughts spun like snowflakes in a blizzard when he thought of Belle and Colton's relationship, and his unrest and dissatisfaction grew.

CHAPTER 4

The men pushed furniture against the walls to free the floor for dancing.

Mom took on the job of emcee. “Okay, everyone, we’re going to start tonight’s entertainment with a country line dance. Mr. Willis? Mr. Joel? Mr. Lewis? Do you know the steps?”

All three said no.

“Miss Morris?”

“Oh, yes. I took lessons.”

“Adam?”

Adam shook his head. “Sorry, Janet, my education in that area has been woefully neglected.”

Liam said he didn’t, but was willing to learn.

“Okay.” Janet pointed. “My husband, sons, and grandsons will stand in a row. Laura, Grace, Belle, Jules, Miss Morris, and the two granddaughters will stand in one next to them. You all will form the third row.

“I’ll call out the steps, and they’ll show you what to do. You copy them, and then we’ll add music after you practice a few times.”

Lewis grinned. “I have two left feet and no sense of rhythm, Mrs. Morgan, so I’ll run the camera.”

Brian laughed when he realized all the Morgan males were dressed in the same type of clothing—black boots, blue jeans, leather belts with large, shiny buckles, and white, long-sleeved western shirts. He hadn't noticed this during dinner or the movie, because too many other, more interesting sights vied for his attention. *I guess you can't take the cowboy out of the cowboys, even for a dance.*

The males had knotted their favorite bandannas around their necks. Brian's blue paisley matched the sapphire color in Juliette's necklace, while Colton's red was the exact shade of Belle's dress. How had this happened? He hadn't known what Jules or the other women would wear.

"Hang on." Dad held up his hand. "We're missing something. Ah. Grab your Stetsons boys. Can't do line dancing without them."

Randy Willis guffawed. "What a sight."

For the next thirty minutes or more, they laughed, stomped, clapped, grapevined, and toe-and-heel tapped their way through the dance.

Brian's blood sang, and energy filled him. This was living.

Mom's eyes sparkled and her cheeks glowed. "Come into the kitchen and grab something cold to drink. The next dance will be slow so we can catch our breaths."

Willis twisted off the cap on a water bottle and sipped. "Thank you, Mrs. Morgan. That was the most fun I've had in a long time.

"I plan to use some of the videos at the end of the documentary so viewers will see Colton, Belle, Liam,

Adam, and the rest of the family together. They will love this.

"Almost a million people all over the world have signed up to be notified of the documentary's release, and a lot of chatter and speculation continues about the book." He took another sip. "Miss Morris?"

Amber turned to him. "Yes?"

"Perhaps we should talk about the timing of the releases. We could help each other."

"That will be Belle and Colton's decision, Mr. Willis, but I'm interested to hear what you have to say."

"Good. Let's talk tomorrow morning."

Mom signaled. "Okay, get ready for the next dance. Because we have more men than women, I'll signal when you should change partners."

Joel approached Juliette, so Brian reached for her hand as they walked into the living room.

When the music started, he pulled her close. "You smell good, Jules."

She grinned. "You do too."

As they moved to the music, Juliette rested her head on his shoulder. He closed his eyes and drew her closer.

When Mother said they needed to change partners, Brian opened his eyes.

Joel stood in front of Juliette, a huge smile on his face. Reluctantly, Brian backed away.

"I believe this dance is yours, brother." Belle slipped into his arms. "Hey, I want to talk to you after our guests leave tomorrow afternoon."

"About?"

She hesitated. "I'll tell you tomorrow."

He leaned back to get a closer look at her face. "This sounds serious. Does Colton know what you want to chat about?"

"Yes, but he won't be present. He doesn't want to influence you one way or the other."

Brian left the round pen with Mindy at his heels when the guests stepped outside with their luggage. He wondered what Belle, Amber, and Randy had decided about the release, and if they planned to work together.

The satisfied looks on all their faces indicated they had come to an agreement.

As much as he wanted to know what this was, he longed even more to know what Belle had on her mind.

"Brian?" Amber stepped forward and held out her hand. "Thank you for welcoming me into your home. I had a delightful time. I especially enjoyed watching you work with the dogs."

He removed his gloves before shaking. "My pleasure, ma'am." *I wish you could stay longer. I'd like to know you better.*

She reached into her shoulder bag. "My business card. My personal cell number is on the back just in case you need to get in touch with me."

He scanned the information, then slipped the card into his back pocket. "Thanks."

"Well, I'm off. I return in a month or two as we wrap things up. Mr. Willis and I will work closely together and release the book and the movie close to the same time. This should create synergy and more overall buzz and interest. Mr. Willis and I have the same flight out, so we'll work on more of the details on the plane."

Brian opened the car door. "I hope to see you again."

Her eyes met his. "Call me. We'll chat."

His heart picked up speed when she smiled at him. She got in, and he closed the door.

Colton and Belle hugged Adam and Liam and followed them to their rental. Colton leaned toward the window and said something. They both nodded and lifted their hands in goodbye.

Brian waved at them, then stepped onto the deck beside Colton and watched all of their guests leave. Now that everyone was gone, his spirit plummeted.

He turned to Belle. "You wanted to talk to me?"

Colton kissed Belle. "I'll be back in a couple of hours, sweetheart. Bill and Charlie need my help with the cattle." His gaze met Brian's. "Later."

"Come into the kitchen, brother. I made us a snack. I seem to be hungry all the time now."

Brian followed her and sat down at the counter. She pushed a glass of iced tea and a plate of fancy sandwiches toward him.

"I'll eat when I've heard what you have to say, Belle. My stomach has been tied in knots anticipating what you're going to tell me."

She laughed and reached for a cucumber sandwich. "I have good news, not bad. I thought about your desire to leave the ranch and do something different, so I talked to my parents. They have a lot of connections, and one of these is a man with a famous art gallery in Dallas. Dad has seen your paintings and loved them.

"I sent photos of the pictures you have hanging in the house. He forwarded them to Mr. Wright, the gallery owner, and he is interested in hosting a showing."

Ice and fire raced through Brian's veins. Someone wanted to host a showing for his paintings? He thought they were good enough?

Brian gulped the iced tea. "When?"

"Within eight weeks if you can be ready. They will need to start advertising the showing immediately if you agree to this. Will Janet and Henry be upset if you take all your paintings from the house and offer them for sale?"

"No." Brian's heart kicked into high gear.

"Do you have more?"

"Yes, in my bedroom. Do you want to see?"

"Of course. Lead the way."

Belle studied each painting with a critical eye. "These should be included with the others, Brian. The clarity and subtlety of each brushstroke, and the way you capture movement and the environment on a flat surface astounds me."

She turned toward the door. "Let's go back to the kitchen and talk over the details."

Brian followed her downstairs and sat at the counter. He reached for several of the different kinds of sandwiches. "I'm suddenly ravenous. Tell me more."

"I have a small studio apartment I bought several years ago. This is close to my folks' place as well as to downtown. You can stay there. The light will be great for painting." She grinned. "Just cover the hardwood floors with a drip cloth before you start."

Shock saturated his system. Belle had just provided him with a way off the ranch and a means to make a living. Love for her exploded inside him, and he jumped up and rounded the counter to lift her in a bear hug. "You're the best sister I've ever had, Belle."

She put her arms around his neck and kissed his cheek. "Don't tell the others, but you're my favorite brother."

He placed her on her feet. "So, what's next?"

She laughed. "Get your paintings together, ship them to Mr. Wright within the next couple of days, say goodbye to your friends and family, and book your flight to Dallas."

"Clothes?"

Belle eyed him from head to toe. "I'm partial to your current cowboy look, but you should be fitted for a tailored suit when you get there. If you're like Colton, you'll hate wearing the ensemble, especially if a tie is involved, but this might come in handy for social events. Ask Mr. Wright's advice as to what you should wear for the showing."

"I don't know what to say, Belle." He stroked her cheek.

She put her hand over his. "Say thank you, and go tell your parents their walls will be bare until you can paint more pictures."

Brian dropped his arm. "You'll come to the showing, won't you?"

"Of course. Colton and I both will. Your parents will come with us. We're family. We need to support each other."

"Thank you, Belle." He kissed her forehead, grabbed more sandwiches, and drained his tea. Joy energized his muscles.

Brian strode to the barn where his folks worked and shared the news.

"I'll be sad when you leave, son," Mom swiped at a tear, "but I've known for a long time you haven't been happy on the ranch." She cupped his cheek. "We'll have a bon voyage party the day after tomorrow. Let your friends know."

Life moved at blinding speed for Brian over the next two days.

He talked with the gallery owner and shipped the paintings, then he booked his flight to Dallas.

Belle watched over his shoulder. "Mom and Dad will pick you up at the airport and take you to dinner before dropping you off at my place. Here, hold out your hand."

Brian turned away from the computer toward Belle. He put out his hand.

She dropped a set of keys in his palm and gave him an envelope. "Keys to my apartment and car. The car is in my assigned space in the parking garage."

He opened the envelope. "What is this?"

"The code to turn off the alarm, directions to Mom and Dad's penthouse, the closest of their restaurants, the location of my favorite gym, the bank I use, the neighborhoods to avoid, the station where you can find the cheapest gas, and the grocery store that has the freshest food. Do you know how to cook?"

"Not like you, but I can manage." He grinned. "Now that the documentary showed me how to fry mice ..."

Belle laughed. "Then I'd advise you to stock up at the market and eat at home. The last several pages are easy-to-make recipes even a Montana cowboy can handle."

He blinked away moisture. "I don't know what to say, Belle."

"You don't have to say anything. Go, and figure out what you want in life."

Though the party was great and the well wishes heartfelt, Brian couldn't settle. Acidic ants crawled in his stomach.

Juliette was the last guest to leave. He turned on the porch lights and followed her to her car. "Thanks for coming, Jules."

She said nothing, but studied his face. In one fluid motion, she stepped close and pulled his face toward hers for a kiss.

As soon as their lips met, Brian wrapped her even closer to him.

She broke away and stroked his face. "Go to Dallas and figure out what life has for you, but don't be surprised if you realize everything you want is back here. Goodbye, Brian."

Her goodbye sounded so—final. The ants in his stomach swarmed as if someone kicked over their hill.

During the next few days, excitement and fear battled for dominance. How well would he be able to function in a totally different environment? Would he be successful? He didn't know what he'd do if he failed. Crawl back to the ranch with his tail between his legs?

No! That wasn't an option. If he returned to the ranch, he wanted to do so with his head high and something to show for his time away. He wanted his brothers and parents to respect and admire him as an individual, not just a family member and skilled ranch hand.

CHAPTER 5

Brian studied himself in the mirror. With his haircut, shave, and suit, he didn't see any sign of the cowboy. Would Amber Morris and his family notice the changes at the showing tonight? How would he look to them?

He adjusted his tie, and the seams at his shoulders and arms strained. His tight collar pinched him. He grimaced. He needed a new jacket and dress shirt. What a pain. He hadn't even worn these once. None of his jeans fit his thighs anymore either, so he'd taken to wearing sweats during the day.

He'd been in Dallas two days, when his body complained about his sedentary lifestyle. Brian enrolled at Belle's favorite gym and, the first day, met a body builder named Ty.

They talked and discovered they liked many of the same things. Their personalities suited, so over the next seven weeks, they worked out. Ty showed him the hows and whys of bodybuilding, and they trained together.

Other than rodeo events, Brian had no interest in competing in contests like Ty trained for, but he liked the man's company, the growing strength in his muscles, and the challenge of doing new things.

He picked up the car keys and reached for his Stetson. *Oops. No hat tonight*. He dropped his hand. He still wasn't used to going outside without head covering. *Guess there's still some cowboy left in me after all*.

He arrived at the gallery with an hour to spare. The staging of his paintings and the way the lighting focused attention on each one took his breath away. They looked much different hanging on a gallery's walls than they did in the lodge or leaning against his bedroom walls.

"You approve?" Dale Wright stopped next to him.

Brian nodded and smiled. "Thank you, Dale. You've shown each piece to advantage."

"You're welcome." The gallery owner studied the painting in front of him. "I'm expecting a stellar turnout tonight. Many from the entertainment world and several private collectors have expressed interest in your work. They sent in their RSVPs early, which is always a good sign."

Brian's gut twinged. He'd been so worried about failure, he hadn't considered what he would do if he was more successful than anticipated. Such success came with greater expectations and demands. Was he ready for them?

Dale turned. "I'm going to check on the drinks and hors d'oeuvres. You said your family will come for the showing?"

"Yes."

He chuckled. "I know them from seeing their faces on so many of your paintings."

Brian's eyes flew to one of the images. "Yes, my brothers are spectacular."

"The one who survived the plane crash will be here with his wife?"

"Yes. So will my parents and a friend who is writing Colton and Belle's story."

"Ah. The book. I've seen a lot of chatter on social media about the upcoming release. I'm thrilled to meet them all."

His folks were the first ones to enter the gallery when they opened the doors to the guests. Dad shook Brian's hand and gripped his shoulder. Mom put her arms around him.

"I'll give you a proper hug when I take off this jacket, Mom. The seams are about to explode."

Dad eyed him. "What happened? You're meatier than when you left."

"I'll tell you later." Brian turned and greeted Colton and Belle.

Belle kissed his cheek and stepped back. "You left the best painting in my room. Why?"

"I gave *Belle's Favorite* to you as a way to say thanks for all your help."

Brian turned to Amber Morris. Adrenaline rushed through him. Beautiful didn't come close to describing her appearance. "Hi, Amber. I'm glad you could come."

She smiled. "I wouldn't miss this for anything. Thanks for inviting me."

His heart pounded behind his ribs, and he had a hard time looking away to greet Belle's parents. The more he'd talked to Amber on the phone since arriving in Dallas, the more her personality drew him. He hoped something more might come of this relationship.

Dale Wright joined them. His eyes gleamed when they rested on Belle and Amber.

Brian introduced him to his family and friends.

Dale pointed to Brian. “You’ve got one talented son here, Mr. and Mrs. Morgan. Not only does he paint amazingly well, but he’s been working with my dog, Ginger.” Wright chuckled. “He discovered that her out-of-control behavior was brought on by her human owners. We didn’t have a clue what to do until Brian showed up.”

Henry nodded. “He’s good with dogs, horses, and cattle, Mr. Wright.”

“I can imagine. He’s popular with some of my friends who also have dogs with issues.” Wright waved them toward the paintings. “Enjoy Brian’s work, then head to the food and drink table. Other guests just arrived, so please excuse me.”

Colton lifted a brow. “Training dogs in your spare time?”

Brian shrugged. “Keeps me in the funds I need to buy canvases and paint.”

Amber touched his wrist. “Will you show me the exhibits?”

“My pleasure, ma’am.” He bent his arm, and she slid her hand into the crook of his elbow. Her nearness and scent scrambled his thoughts.

Within an hour, people packed the gallery.

Brian enjoyed moving around and chatting with celebrities and collectors, though, by the end of the show, he was ready to be out of the spotlight and out of his jacket.

The last guest left, and Dale strode toward him, his smile included Brian's family. "You did amazingly well. Every painting sold. We'll price the next ones higher."

Brian blinked. Higher? He thought the paintings had been priced excessively high.

Dale grinned. "When you have enough for another showing, let me know." He turned to Brian's parents and Belle's and offered his hand. "I'm so glad you all got to come."

More warmth flooded Dale's tone when he spoke to Belle and Amber.

They left the gallery, and Brian immediately removed his jacket and tie. He unbuttoned the first button of his collar and sighed. Blessed relief.

Jackson St. John tilted his head toward the car. "Let's head to our closest restaurant for dessert."

Brian turned to Amber. "Do you want to ride with me?"

"I'd love to. I want to hear more about your dog-training gigs."

He opened the car door for her, then slid into the driver's seat.

On the way to the restaurant, he told her all about his experiences with the dog owners and their animals. "Most of the problems I see are directly or indirectly caused by the humans. They don't understand their dogs' needs and expectations for the breed."

Amber smiled. "So, you have to retrain the humans to fix the dog issues?"

"Correct." He changed lanes. "How is the book coming?"

"Belle approved the edits and cover, so everything is ready for the release. Mr. Willis needs a few more weeks to finish his documentary, but we're ready to move."

Her eyes shone in the streetlights. "His marketing team and ours have already started creating a lot of buzz on social media and television. Mr. Willis is running ads on prime time. Millions are anticipating the release. The numbers of pre-orders indicate the book will be a bestseller."

She laughed. The joy radiating from her encircled him. Today was the best day of his life. The money brought in from the sale of his paintings far exceeded expectations even with the commission he had to share with Dale, and a beautiful woman sat next to him and listened as if his words mattered.

Brian signaled and pulled into the restaurant's parking lot. He tried to calm his racing heart. "Colton said he and Belle would fly to New York City to be interviewed on a television show. I don't know why my brother agreed to such a thing. Since the crash, he doesn't like flying. He also hates big cities."

Amber chuckled. "That's true, but he disliked the idea of Belle going by herself even more."

The others waited for them. After he seated Amber, he pulled out the chair next to her. Her scent kept his senses on high alert.

Brian participated in some of the conversation, but he mostly listened and watched. Would Amber settle into ranch life as well as Belle had, or would she continue to jet around the country in search of more opportunities? Would she be content to stay with a cowboy husband

and children? When he tried to envision this scenario, the kiss Jules gave him blurred and shifted the image.

Doubts filled him. Where did his heart belong?

When he returned to the apartment later that evening, he was too keyed up to sleep. He stripped off his shirt and slacks, then put on his painting clothes.

Brian turned up the air conditioner and examined his latest work. He smiled and glanced at the other two portraits in the series. *Ahh.*

He painted through the rest of the night.

Someone knocked. Brian groaned, then peeked at the clock. 10:00 a.m. He'd slept for four hours, but his body craved a few more. He sighed and pulled on shorts and a muscle shirt.

He opened the door to Belle and Colton.

Colton stared. "Were you still in bed?" The hint of disbelief in his voice wasn't lost on Brian.

"Come in. Yes. I painted all night and went to bed at dawn." He brushed the sleep out of his eyes.

Belle stood in front of the easel.

Brian studied her expression. "I call the three portraits in this series *Elegance*. What do you think?"

Belle studied her image and those of Juliette and Amber. "Is this how you see us? All glamor and shine?"

"Yes."

"We're not, you know."

His brother inhaled sharply, then whistled. "These are spectacular, Brian. You've captured the essence and personality of the women."

Colton's praise soothed some of the deeply buried longing to be accepted by his older brothers.

Brian turned to Belle. "I don't want to sell these, but would you be offended if I showed them?"

"I wouldn't, but you'll have to ask Amber and Juliette. I can't speak for them."

Colton studied Brian's other works, then stopped before a large horizontal painting of the family and friends line dancing at the lodge three months ago. He chuckled. "Look at this, Belle."

She gazed at the image for several moments.

Brian wished he could hear her thoughts.

She turned to him with wide eyes. "I don't know how you captured the sense of energy, movement, laughter, and fun, but you did. I can hear the music and Janet calling out the steps. I can feel our stomps and claps. You are amazing, brother."

Her words were more balm to his soul.

"Thank you." He frowned. "Did you tell me you were coming over this morning? I rode a high yesterday, so I could have missed such details."

Belle laughed. "No, we didn't. We came to take you shopping."

His eyebrows rose, and he glanced at Colton. "Shopping? That's not my favorite thing to do."

His brother tilted his head and eyed him from head to toe. "Mine either, but if you put on any more muscle, you'll burst your seams and embarrass yourself. By the size of your chest, shoulders, arms, thighs, and calves, I bet you can't fit into your regular clothes or boots. Can you?"

Brian grimaced. "I can't, so I wear sweats, shorts, and athletic shoes. Don't tell Dad. This news will offend his cowboy sensibilities. By the way, I'm gifting you all my former clothing and boots, so take them when you go home."

Belle grinned. "Then put on whatever you're going to wear to go shopping. We're lunching with Amber, your folks, and mine at the penthouse, so we'd better find you some clothes and boots that fit, or your secret will be exposed."

"Give me a few minutes to shower." He grinned at Belle. "Make yourself at home." He slapped his forehead. "Oh, I forgot. This *is* your home."

"No, this is my house. My home is with Colton and the Morgan family."

Brian thought about her words throughout the day. The message of "home is where the heart is" niggled and poked at him. If he knew where his heart belonged, he had a chance of figuring out where home was.

Now that his clothes and boots didn't bind him, Brian enjoyed wearing his normal clothing again. He lounged on the couch and inhaled the aroma of good food. *Ah*.

Holly St. John smiled and signaled for them to come. "Grab a plate and silverware at the end of the counter. We're serving ourselves buffet style today. Enjoy."

"The food smells delicious, Holly." Mom turned to Amber. "You'd better go first. You have to catch a flight out this evening."

Brian followed Amber through the buffet line, then sat down next to her.

She glanced at his heaped plate and laughed. "Do you always eat like this?"

"I'm constantly hungry, so I'd say yes." He smiled and unfolded his napkin. "I like your laugh. Tell me something. What makes you so successful at your job?"

She thought for several moments. "I like people, Brian. They interest me."

"Everyone?"

She nodded. "Pretty much. Each person has a story. As a ghostwriter, my job is to listen carefully and pull out the gems."

They ate in silence.

"Do you prefer to work with men or women?"

She chuckled. "Men seem to have a harder time focusing, but I like to work with both."

What man could focus when she looked and smelled so good? She was a real brain scrambler. He dropped his eyes to his plate. "What does your boyfriend think about that?"

Amber grinned. "I haven't asked."

"Will you allow me to drive you to the airport?"

Her eyes met his. "I will."

CHAPTER 6

Brian's cell rang, and he glanced at the number. His eyebrows quirked up and he reached for the phone. "Randy?"

"Hi, Brian. I hear you're getting ready for another showing in two days."

"I am."

"You've been quite prolific in the months you've been in Dallas."

"Yes, sir. How may I help you?"

"I saw the brochure of the paintings to be sold. I'd like to buy the one of us line dancing at the lodge. The picture brings back great memories. I laugh every time I think of our time together. You are selling, correct?"

Brian swished his brush in the jar of turpentine and stood. "I am. The only images I'm not are the portraits of Belle, Amber, and Juliette."

"I saw them. They are astonishing—even more so since I know these women. I'll buy the one of us dancing at whatever price you've set."

"Then I'll reserve this for you. I'll text you Dale Wright's number. He arranges the sales."

They chatted about the showing, then Brian asked about the documentary.

"Belle and Colton have their interview in New York tomorrow to talk about the book. We'll debut the movie in a week, so be sure to watch. I think you'll enjoy the finished product."

Brian chuckled. "I'd like to see my brother in such a large city. He's probably as antsy as a cat on a hot tin roof."

"Belle will keep him calm." Randy laughed. "He's a private man. My guess is he's holed up in his room until time to leave."

"I'll give him a call to see how accurately we predicted."

"Okay. Be sure to tell me what you think once you watch the documentary. This releases in a week."

As soon as they hung up, Brian dialed Colton.

His brother answered on the first ring. "Brian?"

"Hey, I called to see if you and Belle were out on the town."

Colton snorted. "Are you kidding? One big city looks much the same as the others—skyscrapers, too many people, noise, and congested traffic. A man can't breathe here."

"Belle doesn't want to go to the theater or out to dinner?"

"No. She's been to New York City several times and has seen all she wants to see. We're ordering in. Belle is eight months along now and tires more easily. As soon as we finish the interview tomorrow, we're headed home."

Brian laughed. "Randy Willis and I have you figured out. We knew this is what you would do."

"Sorry we couldn't make your showing, man."

"No worries. Bill, Laura, and the kids will represent the family."

"Is Amber coming?"

"No. She's got a lot on her plate right now."

Colton paused. "How often do you chat with her?"

"A few times a week. Why?"

"No reason." The hesitation in Colton's voice focused his attention.

"Is there something you know that I don't?"

Colton sighed. "No. I'm sure if she had anything important to say, she'd tell you."

They talked a few more minutes, then hung up. Something in Colton's tone bothered him. What was up with Amber? His finger hovered above the speed dial number assigned to her.

He pushed the button.

"Brian? Hi." Warmth filled him at the sound of her welcoming voice.

"Hi. I thought I'd check in. See how you're doing."

"I'm ecstatic. Belle's book has already reached number one on the *New York Times Bestsellers List*. I expect she'll sell more in all of the formats after the interview tomorrow."

The genuine excitement in her voice made Brian smile. The way she approached life with interest, energy, and excitement rubbed off on others. "I'm glad. Will you take time off to recuperate before starting your next project?"

She laughed. "Yes. I'll head to the Bahamas soon."

"The Bahamas? You're going alone?"

The line went silent for several moments.

"Amber, are you there?"

When she responded, her voice was low-pitched and serious. "I'm sorry, Brian. I thought you knew. Adam Sutherland and I are getting married. We'll honeymoon in the Bahamas. I sent your invitation to our wedding a week ago."

The room spun, and Brian plopped down in the closest chair. "Married, huh? I didn't realize you even liked the pilot."

"We bonded from the first day we met. He's flown out here several times, and I went to Denver to meet his folks. Over the months, we've stayed in touch. We have a lot in common. We like many of the same things. The wedding is in Denver the last day of September. Your friendship is important to me, Brian, so I hope you can come."

Brian couldn't comment. The sucker punch to his gut left him winded. "Congratulations, Amber. I wish you and Adam life's best. You're two special people."

"Thank you. Your words mean a lot. Please let me know how your showing goes, okay?"

"I will. Goodnight."

"Bye."

Brian walked to the stack of mail waiting for his attention. The invitation lay at the bottom.

He paced the small living room. He couldn't settle. Ty would be with his wife and children now, so he wouldn't suggest they go to the gym.

Brian changed into his workout clothes and grabbed his bag. He'd head to the fight club for some rounds with the punching bag or one of the other fighters in training. He'd started boxing two months ago after Ty's competition schedule required him to be out of town more often.

He enjoyed the change from lifting weights to participating in a more active sport requiring balance, speed, and accuracy. In some aspects, boxing reminded him of competing in rodeo events.

Brian grimaced. He hadn't been on the back of a horse for months. No rodeo for him.

As he took out his frustration on the punching bag, the saner part of his mind questioned why he was so aggravated. *You weren't going out together, were you?*

"No," he muttered and hit the bag with a satisfying thunk.

Did she ever single you out for extra attention over any other man?

Brian thought about the question for a long time. "No, but she made me feel special." He remembered her comment about liking people. Amber made everyone think they were important, even Joel the videographer. He threw several hard punches in a row.

Face the facts. You're not in love with her. Never were. You just appreciate beautiful women.

"Looks like you need to vent, Brian. Get your protective gear on."

Barry, the club owner, tilted his head toward the ring. "Alfonso finished his bout. Says he's willing to go a few rounds with you."

The boxer smiled and motioned to him. "Come, my friend. I will help you to release your anger."

Brian came to his senses in a rush. He could not face a boxer like Alfonso without his mind being in the game. He'd earn a black eye for sure—maybe two. The man was of a similar size and weight but much more skilled.

Brian put on his headgear and mouth guard and took a deep breath. He released all thoughts of Amber and her announcement and focused on the boxer in front of him.

Brian surfed the channels until he found the start of Belle and Colton's interview. He eased onto the sofa and reached for the ice pack. Once the coldness covered the bruise on his ribs, he held another pack to his left eye. Alfonso's punches were as hard as ever.

For the next thirty minutes or more, Brian stared at the screen. The interviewer pulled out a different side of his brother.

Colton had dressed in his best boots, jeans, and western shirt. The red bandanna at his neck and the shiny silver rodeo buckle on his leather belt caused Brian a pang of homesickness. He could almost smell the mountain air and the scent of horses and pine trees.

Belle dressed as elegantly as ever, though the red dress did nothing to hide her pregnancy.

Amber had alternated Belle's chapters with Colton's. At first, she'd intended to tell the story from Belle's point of view, but once she'd visited the ranch and got to know Colton, she'd changed her plans.

Wise decision. The emotion that came to light in the interview helped him better understand what drew Belle to his brother.

The host smiled at Colton. “I’m assuming sleeping arrangements were challenging once Belle admitted her love for you.”

His brother’s jaw tightened, and a muscle moved in his cheeks.

Uh-oh. Brian had seen that expression before. “Keep yourself together, bro.”

Belle touched Colton’s wrist. He took a moment to answer. “Sleeping next to Belle during our struggle always tested my self-control, ma’am, but I’m glad to say I passed each test with my honor intact.”

Good answer!

Would he have had as much ability to resist touching if a woman he loved slept next to him? He squirmed at the thought that Colton, though now less muscled than he, had more strength of character.

The idea nagged at him throughout the next day as he prepared for the showing.

Holly and Jackson St. John were the first to enter the gallery that evening. Holly took one look at his face and gasped before moving aside so he could greet his family.

Bill stared at his swollen eye and the two small butterfly sutures on the cut on his cheekbone. His brother chuckled. “Been brawling, have you?”

Brian grinned. “Boxing. I let my guard slip.”

Landon eyed him. “Did you win, Uncle Brian?”

“No, but I landed more punches than I usually do against that particular fighter.”

Laura kissed his cheek. “The family sends their congratulations.”

Wren tilted her head and scanned his clothes. “You look normal—like a cowboy. Uncle Colton said you’d be wearing a monkey suit similar to the one he wore to your first showing.”

Brian grinned and pointed to his bruise. “I was, but the suit didn’t match the look.”

Christy grasped his hand. “You’re better this way. Will you show us your paintings now?”

“Certainly. Follow me, ladies.”

Brian couldn’t concentrate, so he put his brush down, stood, and paced. He’d had another successful showing, but life seemed ... flat. Empty. He should be rejoicing that he had proven to his family and himself he could survive on his own away from the ranch. Instead, the previous unrest grew. *What’s wrong with me?*

During the next two weeks, he stopped painting and spent more time with friends. He went out to enjoy the nightlife and action, but these also seemed less lively or engaging—like a soda that had been opened and left out overnight.

He vented his frustration in the gym or the ring. At night, he read *Belle and the Mountain Man: An Unlikely Romance.*

On Wednesday, Randy Willis texted to remind him the documentary would show that evening.

Brian turned on the television and found the program.

The movie was the last piece of the Colton-Belle puzzle. As the actors portrayed their survival struggle, information from the interviews and book came together and formed a unified whole.

He now understood why Belle was drawn to his brother—the man and his abilities inspired trust and confidence.

The moviemakers overlaid Liam singing for a couple of the scenes, and the sound of his voice and words of his songs touched Brian's core and magnified the need for something he couldn't identify.

The documentary ended with candid videos of the survivors eating, visiting, and line dancing at the lodge. The celebratory mood lifted his spirit.

He reached for his cell and texted Randy.

BRIAN: Awesome job. You put me into the scenes with the survivors. I was one of them.

RANDY: The ratings are off the chart! Based on the results we're receiving, more than fifty million viewers around the world watched. Can you tell I'm hyped?

Brian congratulated him again and hung up.

The desire for something he couldn't name grew to disturbing proportions.

He walked to the easel and stared at his in-process work. Then, he leaned his newest, finished paintings against the wall and studied them. With the exception of two boxing images and two of Ty lifting weights, all portrayed ranch and cowboy life. *Is this my subconscious telling me to go home?*

Would he be happy returning to Montana and his normal life?

Brian sat and stared at the wall. Scenes from the documentary replayed themselves. Over and over, he heard the words of Liam's songs. He remembered more from the music he'd played and sung at the lodge.

Call him.

Brian frowned. Odd. He reached for his cell and dialed Liam. Maybe the younger man would be out and couldn't answer. He hoped so. Otherwise, he didn't know what he was going to say.

"Hello?"

Brian cleared his throat. "Liam, this is Brian."

"Hi. I've been expecting your call."

"You have?" Brian rubbed his suddenly sweating palms on his jeans.

Liam chuckled. "Yes. I've been praying for you. God impressed on my heart that you're searching. Have you found what you're looking for?"

Brian's heart pounded. "No. Something is missing. How can I rid myself of this hollow feeling?"

His laugh sounded joyful. "Yes. God put that desire in you so you would seek him. He is the only one who can fill your emptiness. Shall I tell you more?"

God? Brian wiped the sweat from his brow and sat. "Yes."

They spoke for hours. Brian ended the conversation on his knees and with tears in his eyes. The emptiness disappeared. Now, if he only knew where his heart belonged. Jules's image popped into his mind, and homesickness flooded his body.

CHAPTER 7

Brian set his bag by the door of Belle's apartment and glanced around. Without his easel and canvases taking up most of the room, the place looked larger.

Once he had decided to leave, he'd taken his finished paintings to Dale to store for another showing in March, then said goodbye to his friends. Now, the only things remaining were to book a flight to Montana and let the family know of his arrival.

His cell rang. *Colton.* "Hello?"

"Brian. We have an emergency here. We need you. Can you come?" The strain in his brother's voice raised the hairs on the back of his neck.

"Yes. What's wrong?"

"Jules and her cousin, Lambert, are missing. They've been pushing cattle out of the mountains for the past few days. Juliette's mount showed up an hour ago. She must have slapped the horse on the rump with a bloody hand because her palm and fingers left a clear imprint."

Brian's heart almost stopped before racing at a frantic pace. *Not Jules!* "The search teams—are they out yet?"

"Family and friends."

"Bill and Charlie?"

"No, they're with hunters and are out of reach for several days.

"The Sheriff's office contacted Search and Rescue. They are on their way. The Blackhawk people are looking, but we need more help." Did panic edge his self-controlled brother's tone?

"Belle is in labor, Brian. She's two weeks early. Her contractions are getting stronger, so I can't leave." Panic definitely flavored his words.

"Talk to Holly and Jackson. Belle just told them about the baby, and they plan to fly out. They'll take you with them."

Brian lifted his bag. "I've already packed and cleaned my stuff out of Belle's apartment. I planned to come home this week. Call Liam and tell him to pray."

Colton said nothing for a handful of heartbeats, surprise evident in his silence. "Done. Mom and Laura will meet you at the airport. Dad's out looking for Jules."

Jackson called the moment Brian hung up. "Meet us at Love Field in an hour. We're taking the corporate jet. The pilot is on his way."

For the next four hours, Brian stared out the jet's window and thought about Juliette. She'd been a part of his life since they were children, and the image of her injured or dying made him sick. What had happened to her and Lambert? Had they gotten crossways with a grizzly or moose?

The moose had started their rut and would be cranky if a rider came too close. The animals especially hated dogs, and Juliette was sure to have a couple of them helping her move the cattle.

A chill crept up Brian's spine. He'd been in an angry moose's sights before and didn't want to repeat the experience.

In his mind, he studied the area where the Blackhawks grazed their cattle. The steep canyons and rough terrain in some of that country would slow searchers if that's where they were.

The more he thought about what needed to be done, the more the acid in his stomach churned. He wanted to be off the plane and on a horse headed to the high country.

Mom and Laura pulled to the curb at the passenger pickup. They hopped out and opened the doors for Holly and Jackson, while Brian lifted the suitcases into the back of the SUV. He shut the door with an impatient hand.

Mom gave him the keys. "You drive. I want to talk to Holly."

Brian started the vehicle and eyed the storm clouds building over the mountain peaks. His heart thumped hard against his ribs. *Great. All we need is bad weather on top of everything else.*

"How's Belle, Janet?" The strain in Holly's words indicated how close she was to tears.

Mom's voice soothed. "The midwife and Grace are with her now. When I left, they were walking around the lodge to try and ease some of the pain. Belle chose a water birth, so she'll get into the tub when the contractions are closer and harder."

As Brian pulled away from the curb, he wondered what Colton was doing. He'd be way out of his element.

When they arrived at the ranch, Brian unloaded the suitcases and strode into the house. He didn't have a moment to lose.

The St. Johns and Mom headed upstairs to check on Belle, while he turned toward the kitchen. Belle's moans and cries could be heard all the way downstairs.

Grace waited for him. "I figured you'd come here first." She tilted her head to the items on the counter. "Your saddlebags are packed with several days' worth of food. I put in the first aid kit plus medicine I mixed for pain. The other jars are labeled with directions for use. The magnesium fire starter as well as matches and your water purification straw are handy. Your canteen is full.

"Dad hitched the trailer and is saddling the horses now. The handheld radios are in the truck fully charged. Extra batteries are in your pack."

"Thanks, Grace." Brian took a pair of jeans, shirt, socks, and underwear from his gym bag and stuffed them into another saddlebag. He stooped and buckled on his spurs, then adjusted his hat.

Dad honked, so Brian slung the saddlebags over his shoulder and grabbed his coat on the way out.

Within thirty minutes of arriving at the ranch, he left again.

Dad turned onto the highway. "The sheriff has a base camp set up on Frank Blackhawk's place. The SAR team should be there soon. The sheriff may call for the dogs and drones."

Brian studied the mountains in the distance. "Any idea where Jules and Lambert are?"

"No. I helped the family look in the place they thought the two should have been, but we saw no sign of them."

"Did Jules's horse return with her rifle?"

He shook his head. "She or Lambert must have removed the weapon from the scabbard."

Relief eased some of Brian's tension.

The Search and Rescue team arrived before they did, so Dad parked out of the way. They walked to the tables where several people gathered.

Jules's father, Frank, saw them, and the stress lines at the sides of his eyes eased. "Henry. Brian. Thank you for coming." He introduced them to Brent Jefferson, the law enforcement officer heading the search.

Jefferson eyed Brian. "You're Colton Morgan's brother? The one who survived the plane crash in Colorado?"

"Yes, sir."

"I read the book and saw the documentary." The officer eyed him from head to toe, then offered his hand. "Good to have you on board. Mr. Blackhawk tells me you have extensive mountain experience."

Brian nodded.

"We need you. We're short on SAR volunteers right now." Jefferson spread open a map marked with grid units. "Gather round people. We have three more hours of daylight, so let's make the best of them."

Once the searchers knew their areas, they tuned their radios to the same frequency and unloaded the horses or ATVs. They checked their packs and climbing equipment and studied maps of their area.

Brian stopped his gelding beside the sheriff. “I have my gear. I’ll camp out each night.”

Jefferson glanced at the bedroll and raincoat tied behind Brian’s saddle and at the bulging bags draped across his pommel. “Okay. You’re teamed with Mason Davis. One of you should check in every couple of hours during the day.”

He nodded. “Will do.”

Brian studied his search partner and liked what he saw. The man was in his late fifties and sat his saddle like he’d been born there. His sun-browned skin and relaxed posture signaled confidence and experience.

Dad squeezed his shoulder. “I have a bad feeling about this whole situation, son. We must find Juliette and Lambert.” He squinted at the sky. “The weather in the mountains will turn soon. Looks like rain.

“I’ll find them if they’re in my area.”

“Be careful, Brian. You chose the roughest terrain to search. That’s moose and grizzly country, so keep your wits about you.”

“I will.” He adjusted his lariat and turned toward the hills.

Brian and Mason rode a zigzag course. They scanned for tracks or any other indication humans or shod horses had recently passed.

The gold quaking aspen leaves whispered in the breeze. Their white trunks seemed to glow as they clustered in front of a backdrop of deep green spruce and pine trees. Had he not been so worried about Juliette and Lambert, Brian could have appreciated the beauty of the fall forest.

They set up a quick camp just before dusk. Mason gathered wood, and Brian started the fire. He radioed their location before pulling out one of Grace's packaged meals.

Mason did the same and heated his food in a small metal pan over the fire. "You know these people?"

"Yes. I grew up with Juliette. Her cousin, Lambert, is eighteen. They've worked cattle from the time they could sit a saddle."

"You think they're lost?"

"No. Hurt, but not lost. They've run cows in this area for years." Verbalizing his fear made the situation worse.

They ate in silence.

Mason opened his thermos and poured a cup of coffee. "What will they do?"

Brian removed his hat and ran a hand through his hair. "Depending on where they are and how severe their injuries, they'll try to get out of the mountains if they can. My concern is the blood. Bears can smell this for miles. They're gorging in preparation for hibernation, which makes me fear for the two.

"Juliette knows how to take care of herself—so does Lambert—but they're no match for a grizzly, especially if one of them is injured. Jules would not have left a bloody handprint on her horse's rump and sent him home if she didn't need help."

His heart pounded to think of all the things that could have gone wrong. He wanted to cry out her name and let the echoes carry his words to her. *I'm coming, Jules. Stay alive, babe.*

"Did the kid's horse show up?"

"No."

"So, they may have a ride out?"

Brian considered the possibility, but his gut told him they didn't. "I don't think so. Jules's message is clear. If they had another horse and could mount, they'd both be riding, and she would not have sent her gelding home."

Mason nodded and said nothing more.

They were in their saddles by dawn and moving slowly uphill. Urgency to find Juliette and Lambert consumed Brian and energized his movements, but he forced himself to remain calm and examine the ground and vegetation with care.

By the end of the day, when they set up camp, they hadn't seen any sign of humans, and Brian's worry increased. None of the other teams had found anything either. He stared into the darkness. *Jules, where are you? How badly are you hurt? Can you last a few more days?*

Mason stirred the fire and sat a mini coffee pot on an equally small grate to boil. "We can at least eliminate the high peaks in the search. If they were moving cattle, they aren't getting themselves in a bind on cliff faces like some of those crazy climbers we've had to rescue." He chuckled and patted his paunch. "I'm glad. I'm not a climber."

Brian sat across from him and pulled another meal out of his pack. "I'm not either."

He chuckled. "By the looks of the slight redness around your left eye and the recent scar on your cheekbone, I'd say you're a cowboy who likes to brawl."

"The cowboy part is right, but the brawling isn't. I took up boxing a few months ago."

"Ah. You let your guard slip."

"Yes."

"Did you land any punches?"

"A few more than I usually do against this fighter."

He eyed Brian in the firelight. "Judging by the amount of muscle straining your shirt, I'm guessing he felt the impact."

"I'm sure he did, but I never know with Alfonso. He doesn't let his pain or emotions show."

"Do you intend to go pro eventually?"

Brian laughed. "No. Boxing and weightlifting were ways I could get exercise while I worked in Dallas."

"What kind of work?"

"I'm an oil painter." Brian reached into his hip pocket and pulled out a folded brochure from his last showing. He handed this to Mason.

The man studied each image. "These are all amazingly good, but the portraits of the women are jaw-dropping. I don't think I could focus, much less breathe, if all three of them were in the same room with me."

Brian nodded. "They are potent when together. The dark-haired one is Juliette Blackhawk—the person we're searching for. The blond is my sister-in-law, Belle, and the other is Amber Morris, Belle's ghostwriter. She will be Mrs. Sutherland in a couple of weeks." The thought didn't cause a jealous twinge, which surprised him.

Mason whistled. “Sutherland. Isn’t that the name of the pilot who survived the plane crash in Colorado with your brother and sister-in-law? I watched the interview and documentary and read the book.”

“Yes.”

“Lucky man.”

Brian agreed and reached for his bedroll.

When the next day yielded no results for any of the searchers, anxiety hit Brian hard. He wanted to call Liam and ask him to pray, but he had no cell service.

Ask me.

Startled, Brian looked around as he unsaddled his horse. He stared into the night sky and whispered, “God. I’m new at praying, so forgive me if I get this all wrong. I need you to show me how to find Juliette and Lambert. Let me get to them soon, and let me find them alive. Please.”

By noon the next day, Brian’s hopes faded and grief choked him. His shoulders slumped.

“Look.” Mason pointed. “Buzzards.”

The carrion birds circled above something ahead and to his left.

Brian dreaded to think what he might find.

Let them be alive.

CHAPTER 8

Brian and Mason rode toward the spot where the birds congregated overhead but stopped at the sound of loud, moaning roars and grunts.

Grizzlies. Fighting.

Chill bumps covered Brian's arms, and adrenaline pumped through his bloodstream. He drew his rifle from the scabbard and chambered a round. He checked the loads in his pistol and replaced the weapon in the holster at his waist.

Mason did the same.

Brian stopped and dismounted. He handed his reins to his search buddy and removed his spurs. "Take the horses to the meadow we just passed. I'll see what the grizzlies are fighting over. Radio our location to the sheriff."

Mason paled. "Stay downwind of them."

"I will." Brian removed a plastic bottle with baking soda from his saddlebag and squeezed some of the powder into the air. The tiny bit of breeze flung the soda behind him. Good. If he didn't make noise, the bears wouldn't smell him.

Wolves howled nearby. *Help, Lord.*

Brian studied the bushes and undergrowth with binoculars before circling to the right and easing toward the sound of conflict.

Sweat drenched him by the time he got close enough to see the carcasses the huge bears fought over. Lambert's horse and one of the Blackhawks' bulls had caused the violent confrontation between the apex predators.

He studied the dead animals from atop a large boulder. Lambert's rope remained looped around what was left of the bull's neck. The tips of his horns were bloodstained. Brian didn't have to see the punctures on the half-eaten horse to know what had happened.

He'd dealt with ornery, aggressive cattle before. Jules probably shot him to stop his attack. That was the only logical explanation he could think of, given the situation, for why such an animal in his prime would be dead.

Jules had cut away the backstraps from both sides of the bull's backbone. Did she suspect they wouldn't be found for several days and had made provision for meat? *Good girl.*

She was smart enough to realize the scent of blood would draw all kinds of undesirables, so where would she go to get away from them?

He scooted to the back of the boulder before rising from his belly and soft footing his way back to his partner.

Mason waited for him, rifle in hands. "Whew. Glad to see you didn't become a bear's meal. Did you find the girl and her cousin?"

"They're in the area." He described what he saw. "My guess is Lambert is injured too badly to ride."

Mason called in the report, but the radio signal was weak and scratchy. They were getting out of range.

The sheriff's reply was unintelligible.

Brian noticed the position of the sun in the sky. *Two hours before dark*. "Hold the horses. I'm going to fire the rifle. Maybe Jules will hear and do the same."

"Let's put more distance between us and those grizzlies first."

They rode thirty minutes to the east and dismounted. Mason led the horses away.

Brian shot twice in quick succession and waited. *Come on, Jules. Answer, babe.*

Someone returned two shots. As close as the shots were together, this would not be a hunter after a game animal, but Juliette. Where had her answer come from?

Brian brushed the sudden tears away and turned east. The sound seemed to have originated from that direction, but he wasn't certain. *She's headed toward civilization.*

Mason eyed the heavy black clouds and pulled out his bright orange rain slicker. "We'd best make camp soon. Looks like we're going to get drenched."

Brian did the same, though he didn't want to make camp. "Let's get in a couple more miles before the rain washes out any tracks."

They had to stop. The sky opened and poured on them.

Brian fired one more time and waited.

The answering shot seemed closer. *Hang on, Jules.*

They built a shelter of pine boughs and huddled under this. Mason started a fire inside and brought out his grill and coffee pot.

Brian shed his raincoat and curled his nose. "I smell as rank as a bull elk in rut." He dug through his bags hoping Grace had packed something to wash with. She had. *Bless her.*

Mason laughed. "The faucets of heaven are turned on full. Enjoy your cold shower."

Brian grinned. "At least the rain isn't icy yet. I'm headed to the creek."

"I'll build up the fire and try to make contact with the command center again."

Brian stripped and scrubbed himself several times and did the same to his shirt and boxers. *Better.* He returned to the overhang, dried, and reached for his clean clothes.

Mason pointed to the twine he'd strung across their shelter. "You can hang them on this."

Brian ate, stretched out on his sleeping bag, and listened to the pops and hisses as his clothes dried over the fire. He interlaced his fingers behind his head and let the sound of the rain lull him.

Tomorrow, God willing, he would find Juliette.

The rain stopped sometime in the night, but the muddy ground sucked at the horses' hooves.

As they rode, Brian tried to put himself into Juliette's mind. She'd choose the easiest path to save Lambert pain, and she'd head for civilization to the east. He scanned the area, then dismounted. “Hang onto the horses. I need to see how far away we are.”

He fired a round and listened intently for a response. The answering shot came from the next canyon over.

His heart swelled. *Thank you.*

They rode closer, and Brian caught the scent of campfire.

Dogs barked when they approached the crude shelter, so Brian whistled and gave the command to hold.

Juliette rushed outside, her eyes wide. “Brian?”

He dismounted, and she flung herself into his arms. “I thought you were in Dallas. Every day after the bull’s attack, I prayed you would come.”

Brian leaned his forehead against hers and drew her close. He brushed away her tears with his thumbs. “Don’t cry, sweetheart. I’m here.”

Mason cleared his throat. “How’s the kid?”

Juliette turned. “Not well. The bull gored his right calf, then pushed his horse against a tree. Lambert’s left leg was caught between the two. I don’t know if the bone is broken, but his leg is swollen.”

“Juliette, meet Mason Davis. He’s with the Search and Rescue.”

“Thank you so much for coming to find us, Mr. Davis.”

The man nodded. “You’re welcome, ma’am.”

Brian removed Grace’s first aid kit and medicine from his saddlebag and ducked under the shelter.

Lambert’s feverish eyes widened when he saw Brian. He smiled. “Hey, man. Are we glad to see you.”

Juliette knelt beside her cousin and unwrapped the makeshift bandage. She grimaced. “I clean this several times a day with hot water, but I don’t like the looks of the wound.”

Brian didn’t either. “Grace packed a bunch of stuff. She said you’d know what to do with what she sent.”

“Thank God for Grace.” Juliette grabbed the kit and read the labels on each container. She opened a bottle with a dropper and sucked up a brownish liquid. “Open your mouth, Lambert. Hold this under your tongue until the medicine is absorbed. You’ll get pain relief and your fever will come down.”

He obeyed while she cleaned the puncture and applied an antiseptic salve. She soaked a cloth in a thick, clear liquid, then put the material on a portion of his swollen leg. She wrapped a bandage around the cloth and covered him with his jacket and hers.

Mason built up the fire.

Juliette nodded. “Thank you. I’ve had a hard time keeping him warm. We’ve been heating rocks at night and putting them next to us. The dogs also curl up beside him, but he’s often chilled.”

Brian opened the other side of his saddlebag and handed the contents to Juliette. “Food. Let’s see if we can get something hot into him.”

Mason nodded and filled the coffee pot with water.

Juliette put on more water to boil in her meal tin. When the water was ready, she dumped in strips of smoked meat and dehydrated vegetables.

Brian smiled. “A fitting end for an ornery bull.”

She looked into his face. “You found the animals?”

"Yes. Two grizzly boars fought to see who would claim the kills. I didn't see any sows, but I'm sure they were around."

Juliette pushed a strand of long, dark hair away from her eyes. "I knew the predators would come, so I decided to move Lambert away from the blood. Otherwise, I'd have stayed put."

After their meal, Mason offered them candy bars. "Do you know where you are, ma'am?"

"Yes, we're fifteen miles from civilization."

He nodded. "In some of the roughest country."

Juliette glanced at Lambert, then turned to Brian with trusting eyes and a gleam of some emotion that sprang from deep inside her. Their gazes met and held for a few seconds before she lowered her lashes.

In that moment, Brian could not define her expression with words because speech left him, but his heart and body had no trouble interpreting her cues. Desire. Longing. Love. Adrenaline raced through his system and fired his muscles.

He swallowed the last bite and reached for his saddlebags. He had to move, or he would explode.

Brian took out a sheathed hunting knife. "I'll cut more branches to add to the roof and sides before the rain starts again."

Mason nodded. "I'll check the horses. They have enough graze and water close by to keep them happy until tomorrow. If we use your lariat and mine, we can make a rope corral."

Brian moved out of the shelter and toward the nearby trees. He eyed the dark thunderheads and wished for sun. If the clouds dumped their heavy loads in a short amount of time, they'd face flash floods and possible mudslides. If the temperature dropped, they'd have snow.

More than anything, Brian wanted to be off the mountain so he could talk to Juliette in private. His heart finally understood that home was a person, not a place. His home was Juliette. He'd never felt this sense with Amber—only energy and drive.

Throughout the afternoon, he and Mason tried to contact the command center with no success. Lightning lit the sky, thunder shook the ground, and the clouds dropped their load.

Mason shook his head. "Too much weather disturbance, and we're out of range."

The dogs whined and huddled near Juliette. She pulled out more of the smoked meat and gave them each a couple of strips. "Sorry, that's all you get today."

She pointed toward Lambert. "Go. Down."

The dogs obeyed and curled up next to him. They watched the humans bring more food out of the saddlebags with focused attention and lip licking.

Juliette reached for Grace's bottles and gave Lambert medicine and some food. She checked his wounds then stroked his cheek and said something Brian couldn't hear.

Her cousin nodded and smiled.

The sight of her gentle touch and the sound of her soft, loving words filled Brian with warmth and longing.

She looked at him in time to see his expression, and her eyes lit.

Am I home to Jules? Do her affectionate glances mean something different to her than they do to me?

The temperature dropped as the sun set. Brian untied his bedroll from the saddle but hesitated to unroll his ground pad and sleeping bag. With the saddles, dogs, and people crowded inside the shelter, space was tight.

Mason unrolled his bedding next to Lambert's right side, displacing the dogs to the bottom of the sleeping bag, so that left Brian to fill the space next to Juliette.

Their eyes met. Brian lifted an eyebrow and waited for her answer to his unspoken question.

She tilted her head toward the small area to her left and moved closer to her cousin.

Brian spread his roll and removed his boots. He eased into the sleeping bag and turned on his side to watch Juliette do the same.

She turned to face him. "Thank you for coming for me."

Brian reached out and caressed the side of her face. "I will always do so."

Her gaze bored into his. "Does that mean you're over your infatuation with Amber?"

"Yes. You knew?"

She smiled. "Of course. Turn onto your back."

Brian did, and she moved to rest her cheek on his right shoulder. She slid her hand across his middle. Though the sleeping bag covered his waist, her touch sent spikes of electricity through him. His arms went around her in an instant.

She whispered, "Your heartbeat and scent comfort me. Belle was right. I know how she felt."

Brian remembered how he'd walked into the hospital room almost a year ago and had seen Belle resting in his brother's arms in the same way Jules rested in his. Now, he fully understood his sister-in-law's words.

He held Juliette and listened to the rain. Mason snored lightly, and Lambert tossed.

Brian continued their whispered conversation. "Jules?"

"Hmm?"

"Do you—" he hesitated, "love me?"

She chuckled and leaned away to better see his face. "For a smart man, you can be oblivious, Brian Morgan. I've loved you since I was a teenager."

He had trouble breathing. "You have?"

She stroked his jaw. "Yes. Your cluelessness played a large part in my decision to leave for two years. What about you? What do you feel for me?"

Several moments passed before he could put his thoughts and feelings into words. "I love you more than my own self, babe. When I heard you were in danger and possibly hurt, my heart almost stopped. I could not envision life without you. Forgive me for being so obtuse."

"You're forgiven."

Brian kissed the top of her head. "When we get home—"

She put a finger over his lips and snuggled closer. "We'll talk later."

Lambert groaned, and Juliette sat up and reached for the medicine.

CHAPTER 9

Brian lifted Lambert to the back of Mason's saddle. The young man made a strangled sound when he straddled the horse's back.

"You okay, man?" Brian didn't like his pallor.

"I'll be fine." He said the words through gritted teeth.

Mason spoke over his shoulder. "If you need to stop, kid, you let me know."

Lambert nodded and grunted.

Juliette's eyes filled with worry. "He doesn't look well."

Brian glanced at the darkening sky. "Let's get him out of here." He mounted and stretched down a hand for her.

She swung up behind him and whistled to the dogs.

They rode for three hours before Lambert cried out, "Stop! I can't go any further."

Juliette slid off the horse and turned toward him.

Brian dismounted and caught her wrist. "Wait, Jules. He's too heavy for you. Let me."

He moved close and held up his arms. "Okay, ease off the horse. I'm ready."

Mason kept his mount still.

Brian grunted when Lambert pushed himself off the horse and fell into his arms. His muscles strained to hold the kid's full weight. Lambert was tall and lean, but he must weigh at least one hundred seventy pounds.

Juliette grabbed her bedroll and pad and pointed. "Put him over here."

Brian got a better hold and moved toward the spot.

Juliette kicked rocks and sticks out of the way, then laid out the bedding.

Lambert moaned when Brian squatted and laid him down.

"Sorry to be so much trouble," he muttered, then accepted the medicine Juliette offered.

Brian stood, and Mason stopped beside him and looked around. "Not a good place to stop. We're too close to grizzly hangouts. I've seen plenty of scat."

"I know." Brian looked at the sky and swallowed his frustration. "I wonder if we can make a travois work?"

Mason frowned. "I don't know how my horse will react to pulling something behind him, but I guess we can give a travois a try."

They cut two aspen saplings to the same length and tapered the ends, then they tied and laced pigging strings to the frame and unrolled Lambert's bedding atop this.

Mason swung into his saddle after the poles were secured. "Let me make a practice run before putting the kid on."

The horse danced a few steps when Mason signaled him to move forward while dragging the travois. His ears flattened and his eyes rolled, but after Mason spoke softly to him and rode up and down the trail a few times, his ears returned forward, and he ignored the dragging sounds behind him.

"Good boy." Mason patted the gelding.

Brian squatted beside Lambert. "Put your arms around my neck and hold on. I'll try not to jostle your legs."

As gently as he could, Brian lifted him and placed him on the travois.

Juliette covered her cousin with her sleeping bag, then mounted behind Brian.

They moved slowly to give Lambert a smooth ride.

Brian figured they covered a couple of miles before they had to stop. A recently downed spruce lay across the trail and blocked their way.

He sighed and dismounted. Mason did the same, and Juliette stood at his horse's head to keep the animal calm and to monitor Lambert.

Brian handed Mason his radio. "Here, hold this. I have a hatchet in my gear. See if you can reach the command center."

As Brian chopped branches, he listened to the scratchy responses. Only a word or two came through on both ends.

Mason indicated the waterfall and rushing stream to his right. "I need to get above the noise. Be back soon."

The top of the tree blocking the trail broke loose just as Mason yelled and slipped on slide rock. He tried to keep his balance, but couldn't. He tumbled down the steep mountainside.

Brian watched the radio fly from his hand and land in the rushing stream. *No!*

He flung the spruce out of the way and moved to stop Mason's fall, but he wasn't in time. The man hit his head against a rock and went limp.

"Mason!" Brian knelt beside him. He stooped and checked for breathing and a heartbeat. His partner lived.

Juliette squatted next to him. "He's bleeding—a lot."

"Yes. Will you bring the bandages Grace sent?"

Without a sound, she rushed to the saddlebags and returned with them, some medicine, and a bed roll.

Mason groaned and opened his eyes.

Brian touched his shoulder. "Don't move. You may have spinal injuries."

He groaned again. "Get the radio off my belt. The thing is poking a hole in my hip."

Brian eased his hand under Mason and pulled out pieces of the radio that had smashed when he landed in a pile of rocks.

Panic choked him.

Both radios destroyed, two seriously wounded people dependent on me to get them home, and ten miles of mountain trails between us and civilization. Don't forget the grizzlies and moose. He'd seen fresh grizzly scat in the trail several yards back. *God, help me, please!*

Juliette sat on Mason's other side. "Stabilize his head while I clean and bandage the wound."

Brian appreciated her sure, gentle movements. He was glad she was here with him.

Mason grimaced. "How bad?"

Juliette's tone remained calm. "You need stitches. I've put extra padding on the wound to add pressure along with some medicine Grace sent to sanitize the cut and staunch the bleeding."

Brian studied Mason's pale face. "Do you have feeling in your hands, fingers, feet, and toes?"

Mason concentrated. "Yes." He wiggled his fingers. "My whole body will be black and blue for a while, but I don't think anything more than my hard head was injured. Help me up."

"No." Brian stopped him. "Don't move. Rest for a bit until we can see if you have more severe injuries."

Juliette covered him with his sleeping bag. "Stay put, mister."

He gave her a weak grin. "Yes, ma'am."

At that moment, thunder shook the ground, and lightning lit the sky. Both horses snorted and rolled their eyes.

Juliette hurried to Mason's horse to keep him from bolting. She stroked his forehead and neck. "Easy, boy. You're okay." She spoke to him for several moments, then checked on Lambert.

Brian gave his horse the same command he gave his dogs when he wanted them to stop. "Hold!" He repeated the order and the horse stilled. He reached for the reins and tied him to a limb.

Mason stared at the sky. "We're going to get drenched here. We need to move."

Juliette chewed on her bottom lip. She looked at Brian. "We'll find cover a few hundred yards from here."

Brian nodded and reached for his hatchet. "Give me a few minutes. We need another travois."

Within fifteen minutes, Brian cut and limbed two nearby aspen saplings and attached them to his gelding.

He used his lariat for the support between the frame and spread his own sleeping pad and bag over this.

Brian stopped his horse as close to Mason as he could, then he and Juliette slid him onto the travois.

"You take the lead, Jules. You know the area better than I do."

She nodded, spoke to Lambert, then signaled the dogs to follow.

They led the horses and kept a slow pace. When they reached the place Juliette mentioned, she pointed to a shallow cavern at the base of a rocky ledge. "The space isn't large, but we'll be mostly out of the weather."

With great care, they laid Mason and Lambert side-by-side on the sandy floor after the pads were placed and covered them with their sleeping bags.

Lambert shivered, and Juliette unzipped her bag and placed this over him.

Brian removed the saddles and travois from the horses and dropped the canteens and saddlebags next to Juliette. "I'll be back soon. I'm going to water the animals and stake them on that patch of grass over there. I'll take the dogs with me."

"Okay. I'll get a fire going and start lunch."

He smiled. "I'm glad you're here."

Her eyes lit. "I'm glad *you're* here. You give me hope."

Hope. He hoped for a lot of things, and they all revolved around this woman.

The wind picked up, and Brian raised the collar of his jacket.

Once the horses were watered and staked, Brian brought more branches to lean against the mouth of their shelter and cut firewood. The cold wind chilled any exposed skin. He sniffed the air. At this elevation and time of year, snow could accumulate if a front moved through.

Brian ducked under the overhang and squatted by the fire to warm his hands.

Juliette must have fed Lambert and given him medicine, because he slept.

Mason wanted food and drink, but Juliette hesitated. "You'd best not have anything until we know how badly you're hurt."

"I'm bone dry, ma'am."

"Then give me your bandanna. I'll dampen this and you can wet your lips."

He sucked at the moisture, then she wiped his forehead with the cloth.

Brian filled four aluminum plates and sat two of them before the dogs. They wolfed the food. He handed the other to Juliette.

They ate in silence.

Mason groaned, rolled to an elbow, and vomited onto the sand. The stench filled the small space.

Juliette dampened his bandanna again and washed his face. She gave him enough water to rinse the taste out of his mouth.

Brian reached for his hatchet, dug a hole, and pushed the mess in with a stick. He covered this with sand.

Mason rolled to his back and closed his eyes. "Sorry."

Juliette felt his forehead. "Don't be. You have a concussion. Vomiting comes with the territory."

For the next few hours, Brian and Juliette sat under the overhang and listened to the rain and the groans.

Brian took off his hat and pinched the skin between his eyes. "Jules, if the weather clears tomorrow, I need to ride out to find help. The command center is ten miles away."

Juliette's eyes widened. "I don't want to be left here by myself with two injured men in grizzly country. What if they get worse while you're gone? I'm scared, Brian."

"Maybe you should ride out and I'll stay."

She chewed on her bottom lip for several moments. Slowly, she shook her head. "You'd be here at least another day. We'll be out of food soon, and the guys need help now."

He put his arm around her and drew her close. She leaned her head against his shoulder, and they sat like that until the dogs jumped up, bodies tense and hackles raised. They snarled and growled at something in the trees nearby.

Brian grabbed his rifle, and Juliette did the same. He scrambled from under the overhang, she only a step behind.

In the fading light, a young grizzly stepped from between the trunks and lifted his head, his nostrils moving to catch any scent. He stood and stared at the dogs, then dropped to all fours and lumbered toward camp. Without a doubt, he could smell the food they'd cooked.

Brian slid the safety on his rifle to the off position and waited, his finger near the trigger. *Don't come closer, bear.*

Both dogs rushed toward the predator and harassed him. One took the front and side positions, while the other worked from the back and moved to the other side when necessary. They barked, snarled, lunged, and nipped until the disgruntled bear had enough and spun away to retreat into the forest.

Juliette called the blue healer and border collie to her and checked them for injuries, then she patted and praised.

The dogs' self-satisfied postures brought a grin to Brian's lips.

Juliette's eyes met his. "We'll put the men on the travois as we did today, but no one stays behind tomorrow."

Brian nodded. "We leave together."

Juliette unrolled her sleeping pad next to Lambert and tilted her head toward the space next to her. "Unzip your bag. We'll have to share."

He did, then sat down and removed his boots. He eyed the dogs standing guard at the mouth of the overhang and relaxed.

Juliette checked on Mason and Lambert once more before removing her boots and sliding in beside him.

He covered them with his bag.

Without a word, Juliette turned and rested her cheek on his shoulder and draped an arm across his middle. She stroked his side. Her warmth collided with his.

Brian's arm went around her, but he forced his hands to remain still as her scent filled the space. His breathing turned shallow, his heart raced, and every nerve ending in his body fired.

He forced himself to inhale and exhale slowly. He remembered Belle and Colton's interview, where his brother admitted that sleeping next to the woman he loved tested his self-control, but that he'd passed each test with his honor intact.

Honor—a synonym for honesty, integrity, and uprightness. Brian wanted to be such a person, to be the kind of man God expected, but the overwhelming desire Juliette's touch created rebelled against the restraints honor demanded.

He struggled until he heard her deep, even breathing, then eased his arm out from under her and turned on his side.

Brian's heartbeat returned to normal, and he sighed. He'd passed this test and could stand next to Colton with his head held high, though he suspected the next test of his self-control would be as difficult.

CHAPTER 10

Brian woke to the sound of a high-pitched engine. He raced into his boots and hat and squinted at the clear sky. A drone flew to the west of him.

"Here." Mason fumbled for his pack and pulled out a flare gun.

Brian's eyebrows raised. They'd had the signaling device all along? His mouth tightened, but he didn't waste time with questions or recriminations. He lifted his arm and fired the flare.

The drone turned east toward them and circled several times before dipping a wing and disappearing over the treetops toward the command center.

Juliette smiled and shaded her eyes. "They know where we are."

He put an arm around her and drew her close. "We need to talk when we get home, babe."

"Yes, we will. Right now, let's eat breakfast. Lambert has better color, and Mason won't stay down."

They ate the last of their food and packed their things. Juliette insisted Mason rest until help came. He grumbled, but did as she ordered.

Brian wasn't surprised to hear riders approaching four hours later, but he was startled to see his three elder brothers riding up the trail toward them.

He grinned when they dismounted near the overhang. "Did you ditch the hunters and the baby?"

Colton's eyes lit. "No to both questions. The hunters filled their tags early, so Bill and Charlie brought them and their meat in. The women have Belle and my son well in hand."

Brian clapped Colton's shoulder. "A boy? Congratulations, bro. What did you call him?"

"Hunter. Hunter Zane Morgan."

Charlie laughed. "He eats like there's no tomorrow."

Bill smirked. "Yeah, just like his daddy."

Juliette hugged them. "I'm so happy to see you boys."

Bill studied her face, and his tone sobered. "We're glad to find all of you alive, Jules. Everyone has been concerned these last few days."

Colton looked past her to the pallet. "How's Lambert."

"Better today, though he isn't going to be able to ride out."

Bill squatted next to her cousin and glanced at the bandages on his legs. "The helicopter with the medics on board will be here soon, so hang on."

Lambert smiled. "That should be an interesting ride."

Mason stood and slung his saddlebags over his shoulder, but the movement made him grimace.

Brian introduced him, and Mason nodded and studied each of them. He looked at Colton the longest.

Bill eyed Mason's head bandage. "You okay?"

He shrugged. "Got a concussion when I rolled down the mountain and landed in a pile of rocks."

Charlie frowned. "You'd better not push your luck then. Why don't you sit down and wait for the paramedics to get here?"

He nodded, but his body language indicated his displeasure at having to do so.

While they waited for help, Juliette told about their misadventures, and Lambert added details. Then, Brian related his and Mason's part of the story.

The helicopter arrived twenty minutes later and landed in a nearby meadow.

A man and woman wearing paramedic uniforms exited the chopper with medical bags and a stretcher. They introduced themselves, then knelt beside Lambert, asked many questions, checked his vitals, then removed the bandages and studied his injuries. They braced his left leg, and cleaned and rebandaged his right before moving him onto the stretcher and carrying him to the helicopter.

The woman returned and walked toward Mason. "I'd like to look at your head, sir."

Mason described his fall down the mountain as she unwound the bandage and examined the wound. She checked his pupils, motor function, and sensory responses. "Just to be safe, I'd like to put you in this cervical collar to stabilize your neck."

"Check his right hip too. He landed on the radio." Brian motioned, and he and the others turned away to give the two some privacy.

When the medics wanted Mason to get into the helicopter, he said he was fine and would ride back.

The woman shook her head and said in a firm tone, “That would be ill-advised, Mr. Davis.”

Juliette slipped up next to him and put her hand over his. She spoke to him in a soft, musical voice. Her dark eyes smiled. “Will you do this for me, Mason? I don’t want Lambert going by himself. I’ll ride your horse down and make sure he’s cared for. Please?”

Mason’s eyes widened. He blinked and stared at Juliette for several moments. “Okay, ma’am. I’ll go with them and keep an eye on your cousin.”

Brian chuckled under his breath to see how dazed Mason looked after Jules stepped into his space. Her beauty captivated and sucked words out of most men’s mouths, including his.

The chopper left, and Brian, Juliette, and his brothers mounted and rode toward the command center. They made the ten miles in three-and-a-half hours.

His dad’s welcoming smile grew when they rode to the horse trailer and dismounted. He clapped each of their shoulders and hugged Juliette.

Frank Blackhawk waited a step behind, tears in his eyes. He embraced Juliette and wanted to know details about Lambert.

Brian watched and listened to her as he unsaddled. The rhythm of his heart increased, and adrenaline pumped through his blood. Jules loved him. Did this mean she would accept his marriage proposal when he offered?

His mouth dried. *Marriage. A wife. Am I ready?*

His gut felt like he'd swallowed live snakes. He'd be responsible for the welfare of Jules and any children they had—at least, that's how things worked in the Morgan family. Did he have the necessary skills to be the kind of husband she needed? To be a good father?

The snakes twisted and roiled. He needed to talk to his brothers soon. They made marriage and fatherhood look easy, though he knew they had ups and downs like everybody else.

His panic eased. If Colton could do this, then Brian figured he could too. His jaw firmed.

Juliette turned to him and smiled, the look in her eyes soft and full of love. The snakes stopped writhing, and he strode toward her.

Brian hadn't seen Juliette for a week, though they'd texted, and his impatience grew. Every time he tried to make a date, he was called away to help his brothers fix fences, take care of elk hunters, or hold his nephew while Belle cooked, like he did now.

He stared at the baby in his arms. Brian didn't mind the last task, as long as Belle didn't ask him to change his diaper, because the baby fascinated him.

Colton entered and hung his hat on a hook. He kissed Belle, then walked toward Brian, spurs jingling, and a smile stretching the corners of his lips.

"What's so funny?"

Colton laughed. "You look like Goliath cuddling a kitten. Hey, how about you babysit for Belle and me this Friday, while we grab dinner and a movie in town?

The others are occupied but will be around if you need help. Of course, you'll have to learn to change Hunter's diaper."

Belle chuckled. "Yes, Colton can teach you."

His brother paled under his tan but nodded. He held out his arms, and Brian transferred Hunter.

Brian stroked the baby's cheek with a finger. "Can you make your date for Saturday? I want to take Juliette out Friday."

Colton's eyebrows lifted. "Are you going to ask her to marry you?"

Heat rushed up Brian's neck, and he grimaced. "Yes, bro, if I can get away from cows, fencing, and woodcutting long enough to ask."

His phone dinged. He read the message and smiled. "Jules said she'd come."

Colton slapped his shoulder. "Okay. You're on babysitting duty Saturday evening then."

Uncertainty flooded Brian. Had he bitten off more than he could chew? Why hadn't he paid more attention to how to care for a baby when his nieces and nephews were small? He swallowed hard, and his insides trembled.

Brian knocked on Juliette's front door and waited, flowers in hand. Nerves twisted his middle so hard, he hadn't been able to eat all day.

She opened the door, and words left him. He stared at the supermodel standing before him. How could he be so lucky?

Juliette grinned. “Are the roses for me?”

The tops of his ears heated as he handed her the bouquet. “You look fabulous, Jules. I always liked that color of blue on you.”

She scanned him from head to toe and gave him a teasing smile. “You’re quite stunning yourself, cowboy.” She signaled him inside. “Let me put these in a vase and grab my jacket. Be right back.”

Frank eyed him from his leather easy chair. “All gussied up for a party, are you?”

Brian approached and sat on the sofa across from Juliette’s dad. “Hey, Frank. I want to ask your daughter to marry me tonight. Are you okay with this?”

He said nothing for several moments, then stood and held out his hand. “You left Dallas to look for my girl, and you brought her home alive. She’s loved you for a long time, so don’t you go breaking her heart, you hear me?”

Brian stood and accepted the handshake. “I won’t.”

“Then, welcome to the Blackhawk family.”

Brian interlaced his fingers with Juliette’s as they walked down the busy sidewalk and breathed in the crisp night air. The slight breeze soughed through the tree branches. “Let’s stop at the park before heading to the restaurant, okay?”

She nodded, and he led her across the street to a park bench and sat after she did. “Thanks. I don’t think I can eat anything until I hear your answers to a couple of questions.”

One of her dark eyebrows rose, and a grin turned up the corners of her lips. She rested her hand on his bicep. "Then, ask. I'd hate for you to waste away to nothing."

He caressed her face. "I love you, Jules. Will you marry me?"

She said nothing, but her eyes smiled. She stroked his cheek and jaw and traced her fingers across his lips. "Yes."

Her touch set him on fire. "Come here." He wrapped his arms around her and pulled her close. Her kisses were as hungry as his.

Juliette encircled his neck with one arm to pull him closer, then buried the fingers of the other hand in his hair. He lost his sense of time and place. Home beckoned.

Eventually, she opened her eyes and leaned back to see his face. "What's the second question?"

A muscle in Brian's jaw tightened, and he shook his head. "I agreed to babysit Hunter tomorrow evening so Belle and Colton can have a night out. I don't know what I was thinking.

"Colton tried to teach me how to change a dirty diaper, but we gagged and choked so much, Belle finally rescued us."

Juliette laughed. "I wish I could have seen that. Two big, tough cowboys stymied by a poopy diaper."

"The experience wasn't pleasant, Jules. My hands shook the whole time. The odor was awful. I think I can still smell the stench even now." He swallowed hard and fought to squelch his gag reflex.

She laughed harder and wiped at tears.

He grasped her wrists. "You've had a lot of experience tending babies in your family, so would you put me out of my misery and say you'll come over and help?"

She tilted her head and pursed her lips as if trying not to laugh. "I'll come over on one condition."

Brian recognized the mischief in her eyes and hesitated. "And that is?"

Juliette snuggled closer and laid her head against his chest. "You continue to practice changing Hunter's diapers so you are a master by the time our babies come."

Our babies? His arms tightened around her. Streams of fire and ice pumped into Brian's bloodstream, and his breathing turned shallow. Did she hear how fast his heart pounded?

The future rushed toward him at an alarming speed. Quick snapshots of his life with her flashed through his mind—Juliette working beside him in the day and sleeping in his arms at night. Juliette pregnant with his child, then rocking their newborn to sleep. Their son or daughter growing up in a large family surrounded by people who will love them and teach them important things about life and living on a ranch. His little cowboy or cowgirl. The vision took his breath away.

She pulled back to look into his face. "Deal?"

He focused on her smile. What had they been talking about?

Juliette laughed. "Hunter. Diapers. You becoming a master changer?"

"Ah." He sighed. "Yes, we have a deal, though I may have to invest in a hazmat suit and gas mask."

Her deep, amused laugh invited him to join her. His laugh came from deep inside. Life was good. Life was exciting. He stood, pulled her up, and entwined their fingers. “Let’s eat, love. I’m starving.”

ABOUT THE AUTHOR

DERINDA BABCOCK is an author and graphic designer. She lives in southwestern Colorado near the base of the western slope of the Rocky Mountains. In her previous career as an English as a Second Language teacher, she worked with students of all ages and many different linguistic and cultural backgrounds. The richness of this experience lends flavor and voice to the stories she writes. You can contact her at www.derindababcock.com/contact

THE
JINDENTORS
A TALE OF THREE KINGDOMS
BOOK 1
DERINDA BABCOCK

THE
VINDORANS
A TALE OF THREE KINGDOMS
BOOK 2
DERINDA BABCOCK

THE
BINROMESE
A TALE OF THREE KINGDOMS
BOOK 3
DERINDA BABCOCK

DODGING DESTINY
DESTINY SERIES BOOK 1
THIRD EDITION
DERINDA BABCOCK

IN SEARCH OF
DESTINY
DESTINY SERIES BOOK 2
THIRD EDITION
DERINDA BABCOCK

DESTINY TRILOGY BOOK 3
FOLLOWING
DESTINY
DERINDA BABCOCK

HUNTING FOR
DESTINY
A DESTINY TRILOGY
NOVELLA
DERINDA BABCOCK

VOICES FROM THE
PAST
A DESTINY TRILOGY
CHRISTMAS SHORT STORY
DERINDA BABCOCK

TREASURES OF THE HEART BOOK 1
COLORADO
TREASURE
DERINDA BABCOCK

TROUBLE
IN TEXAS
COMING
DERINDA BABCOCK

THE PRODIGAL
RETURNS
COMING
DERINDA BABCOCK

THINGS
NOT SEEN
DERINDA BABCOCK

DERINDA'S OTHER BOOKS

A TALE OF THREE KINGDOMS SERIES

The Jindentors (audiobook available), Book 1

The Vindorans, (audiobook available) Book 2

The Binromese, Book 3

THE DESTINY SERIES

Dodging Destiny (audiobook available), Book 1

In Search of Destiny, Book 2

Following Destiny, Book 3

Hunting for Destiny (novella), Book 4

Voices from the Past (short story), Book 5

TREASURES OF THE HEART TRILOGY:

Colorado Treasure (audiobook available), Book 1

Trouble in Texas (coming soon), Book 2

The Prodigal Returns (coming soon), Book 3

Lawmen, Soldiers, & Other Heroes: A Romance Collection

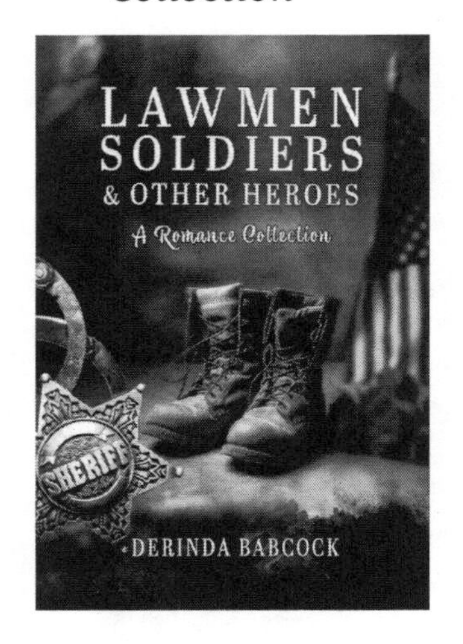

NOTE TO READER

If you enjoyed *Things Hoped For*, please post an online review on Amazon and/or Goodreads. Thanks! Your opinion matters.

Made in the USA
Middletown, DE
26 August 2024

59375367R00062